GOSCINNY AND UDERZO

PRESENT

An Asterix Adventure

ASTERIX
AND THE
GREAT DIVIDE

Written and Illustrated by ALBERT UDERZO

Translated by ANTHEA BELL *and* DEREK HOCKRIDGE

ORION

Asterix titles available now

1 Asterix the Gaul
2 Asterix and the Golden Sickle
3 Asterix and the Goths
4 Asterix the Gladiator
5 Asterix and the Banquet
6 Asterix and Cleopatra
7 Asterix and the Big Fight
8 Asterix in Britain
9 Asterix and the Normans
10 Asterix the Legionary
11 Asterix and the Chieftain's Shield
12 Asterix at the Olympic Games
13 Asterix and the Cauldron
14 Asterix in Spain
15 Asterix and the Roman Agent
16 Asterix in Switzerland
17 The Mansions of the Gods
18 Asterix and the Laurel Wreath
19 Asterix and the Soothsayer
20 Asterix in Corsica
21 Asterix and Caesar's Gift
22 Asterix and the Great Crossing
23 Obelix and Co.
24 Asterix in Belgium
25 Asterix and the Great Divide
26 Asterix and the Black Gold
27 Asterix and Son
28 Asterix and the Magic Carpet
29 Asterix and the Secret Weapon
30 Asterix and Obelix All at Sea
31 Asterix and the Actress

Asterix and the Class Act

Coming soon

Asterix versus Caesar
The Twelve Tasks of Asterix
Asterix Conquers America
Operation Getafix

Original title: *Le Grand Fossé*

Reprinted in November 2004

Exclusive Licensee: Orion Publishing Group
Translators: Anthea Bell and Derek Hockridge
Typography: Bryony Newhouse

This edition first published in 2001 by Orion Books Ltd
Orion House, 5 Upper St Martin's Lane, London WC2H 9EA

Printed in Italy

http://gb.asterix.com
www.orionbooks.co.uk

A CIP catalogue record for this book is available from the British Library

ISBN 0 75284 712 0 (cased)
ISBN 0 75284 773 2 (paperback)

Distributed in the United States of America by Sterling Publishing Co., Inc.
387 Park Avenue South, New York, NY 10016-8810

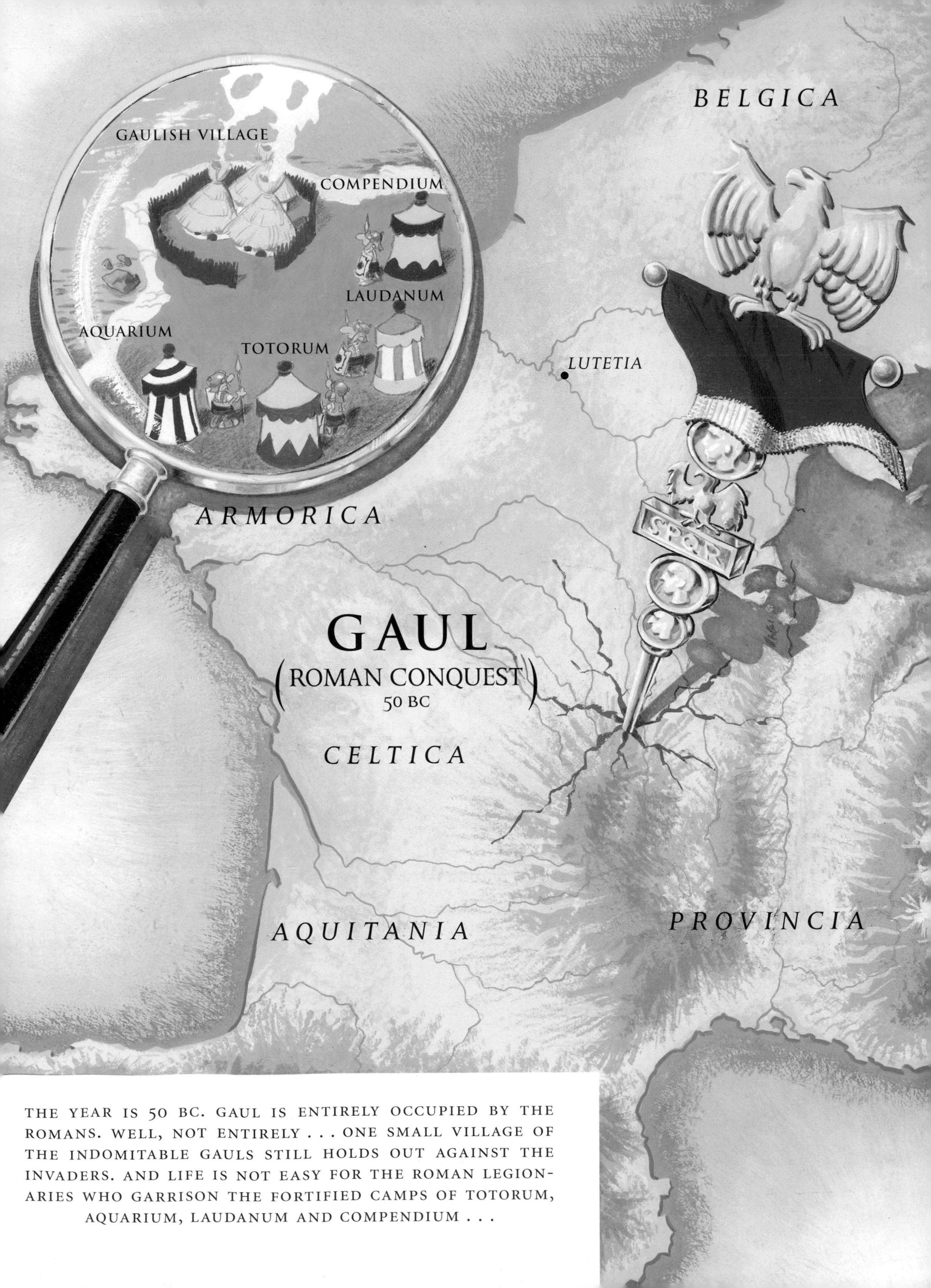
BELGICA
GAULISH VILLAGE
COMPENDIUM
LAUDANUM
AQUARIUM
TOTORUM
LUTETIA
SPQR
ARMORICA
GAUL
(ROMAN CONQUEST)
50 BC
CELTICA
AQUITANIA
PROVINCIA

THE YEAR IS 50 BC. GAUL IS ENTIRELY OCCUPIED BY THE ROMANS. WELL, NOT ENTIRELY . . . ONE SMALL VILLAGE OF THE INDOMITABLE GAULS STILL HOLDS OUT AGAINST THE INVADERS. AND LIFE IS NOT EASY FOR THE ROMAN LEGIONARIES WHO GARRISON THE FORTIFIED CAMPS OF TOTORUM, AQUARIUM, LAUDANUM AND COMPENDIUM . . .

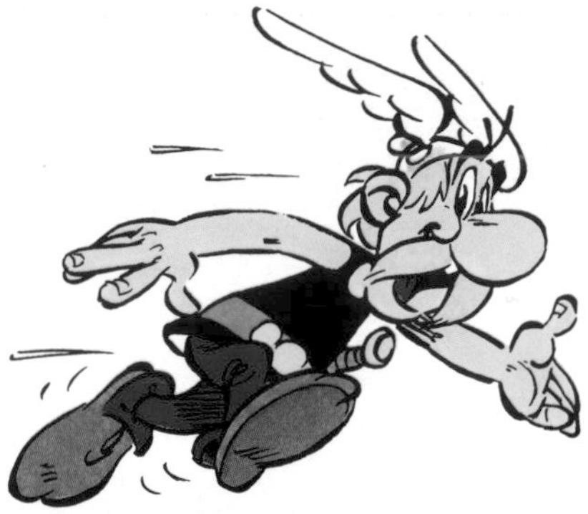

ASTERIX, THE HERO OF THESE ADVENTURES. A SHREWD, CUNNING LITTLE WARRIOR, ALL PERILOUS MISSIONS ARE IMMEDIATELY ENTRUSTED TO HIM. ASTERIX GETS HIS SUPERHUMAN STRENGTH FROM THE MAGIC POTION BREWED BY THE DRUID GETAFIX . . .

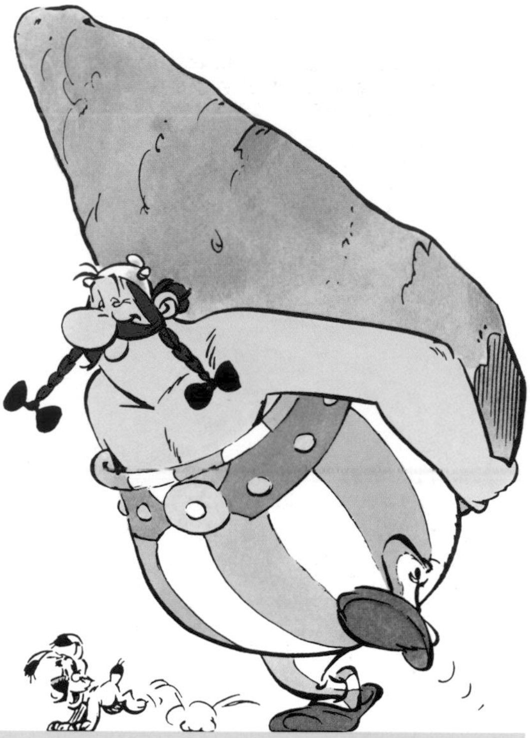

OBELIX, ASTERIX'S INSEPARABLE FRIEND. A MENHIR DELIVERY-MAN BY TRADE, ADDICTED TO WILD BOAR. OBELIX IS ALWAYS READY TO DROP EVERYTHING AND GO OFF ON A NEW ADVENTURE WITH ASTERIX – SO LONG AS THERE'S WILD BOAR TO EAT, AND PLENTY OF FIGHTING. HIS CONSTANT COMPANION IS DOGMATIX, THE ONLY KNOWN CANINE ECOLOGIST, WHO HOWLS WITH DESPAIR WHEN A TREE IS CUT DOWN.

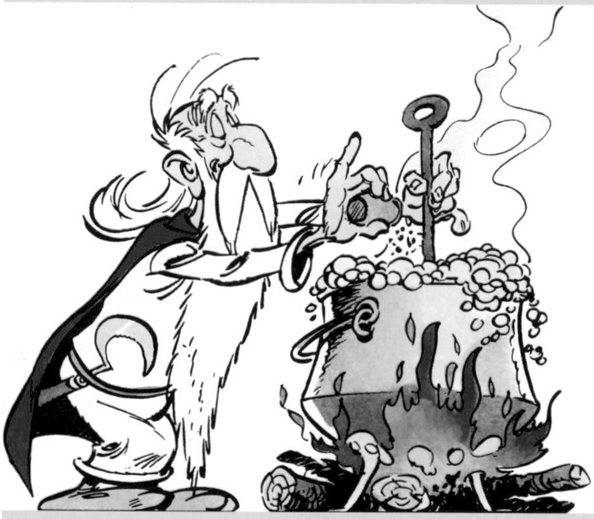

GETAFIX, THE VENERABLE VILLAGE DRUID, GATHERS MISTLETOE AND BREWS MAGIC POTIONS. HIS SPECIALITY IS THE POTION WHICH GIVES THE DRINKER SUPERHUMAN STRENGTH. BUT GETAFIX ALSO HAS OTHER RECIPES UP HIS SLEEVE . . .

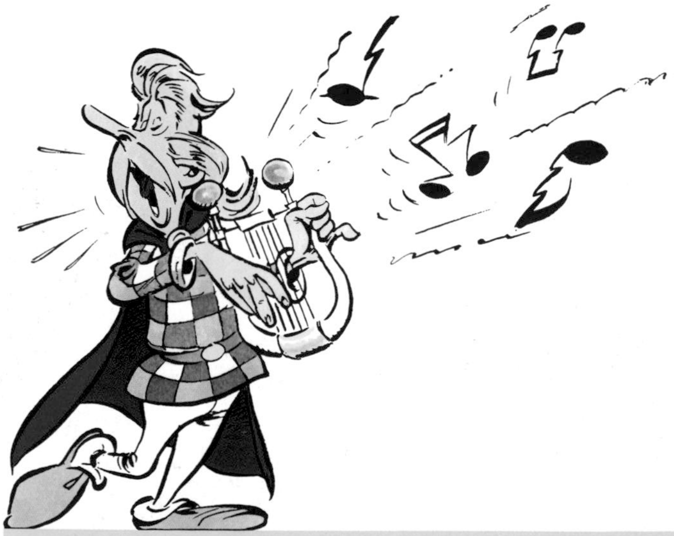

CACOFONIX, THE BARD. OPINION IS DIVIDED AS TO HIS MUSICAL GIFTS. CACOFONIX THINKS HE'S A GENIUS. EVERYONE ELSE THINKS HE'S UNSPEAKABLE. BUT SO LONG AS HE DOESN'T SPEAK, LET ALONE SING, EVERYBODY LIKES HIM . . .

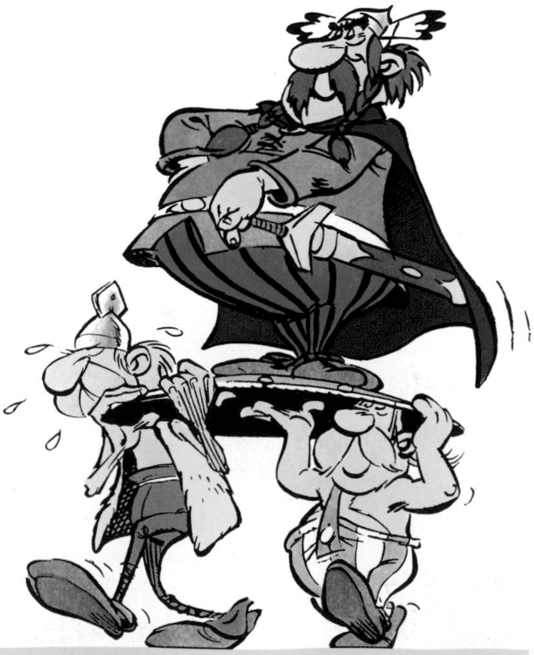

FINALLY, VITALSTATISTIX, THE CHIEF OF THE TRIBE. MAJESTIC, BRAVE AND HOT-TEMPERED, THE OLD WARRIOR IS RESPECTED BY HIS MEN AND FEARED BY HIS ENEMIES. VITALSTATISTIX HIMSELF HAS ONLY ONE FEAR, HE IS AFRAID THE SKY MAY FALL ON HIS HEAD TOMORROW. BUT AS HE ALWAYS SAYS, TOMORROW NEVER COMES.

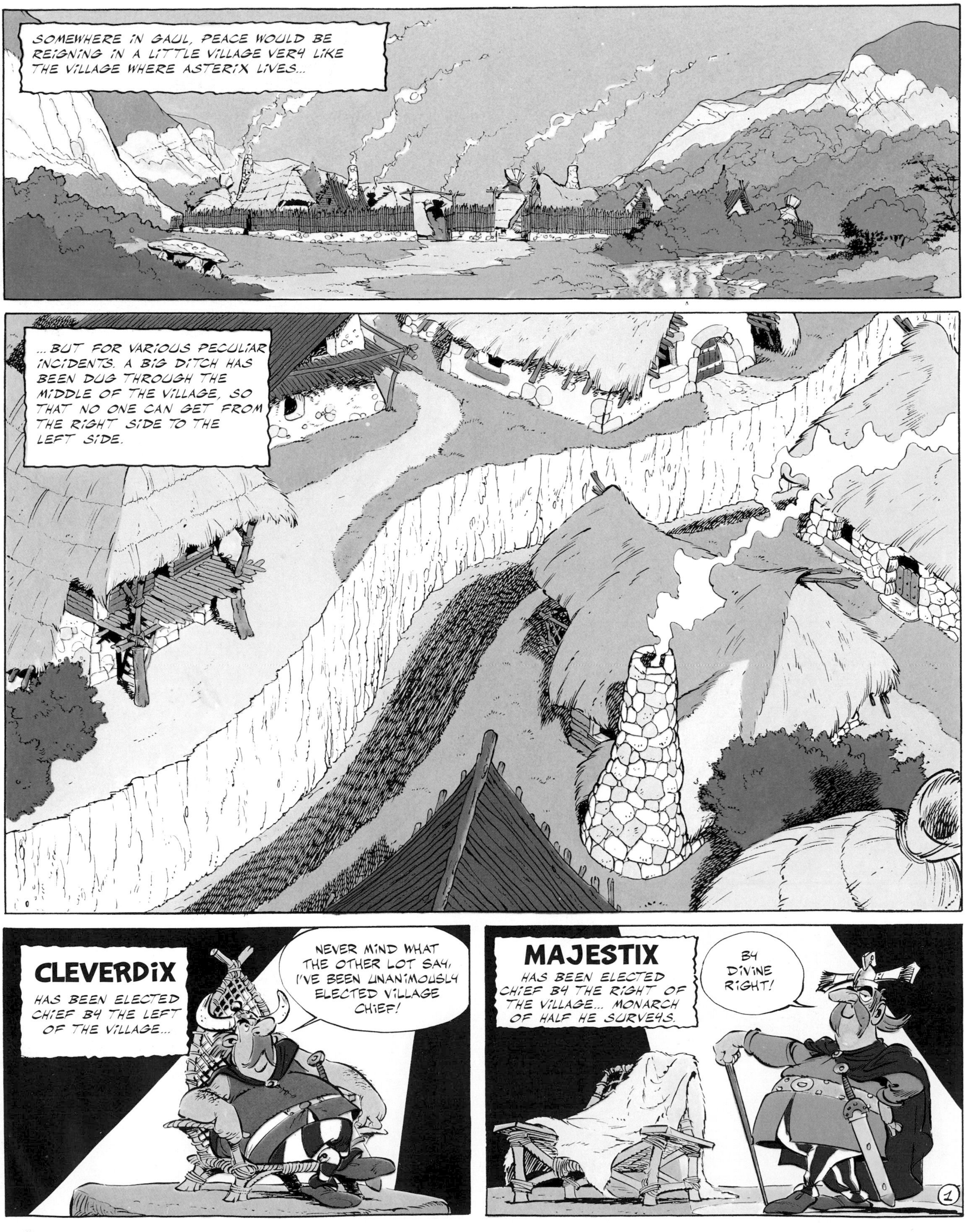

SOMEWHERE IN GAUL, PEACE WOULD BE REIGNING IN A LITTLE VILLAGE VERY LIKE THE VILLAGE WHERE ASTERIX LIVES...
...BUT FOR VARIOUS PECULIAR INCIDENTS. A BIG DITCH HAS BEEN DUG THROUGH THE MIDDLE OF THE VILLAGE, SO THAT NO ONE CAN GET FROM THE RIGHT SIDE TO THE LEFT SIDE.
CLEVERDIX HAS BEEN ELECTED CHIEF BY THE LEFT OF THE VILLAGE...
NEVER MIND WHAT THE OTHER LOT SAY, I'VE BEEN UNANIMOUSLY ELECTED VILLAGE CHIEF!
MAJESTIX HAS BEEN ELECTED CHIEF BY THE RIGHT OF THE VILLAGE... MONARCH OF HALF HE SURVEYS.
BY DIVINE RIGHT!
1

VARIOUS ATTEMPTS HAVE BEEN MADE TO DEAL WITH THE SITUATION ...

AND THE VILLAGERS OF THE LEFT AND THE RIGHT ARE EVER READY TO EXPRESS THEIR MUTUAL ANTAGONISM.

RSPRR! RSPRR!

BUT IT WOULD TAKE POSITIVELY SINISTER DEXTERITY TO SOLVE CERTAIN VITAL PROBLEMS ...

?!

?!

...AND ONLY THE CHILDREN ARE ANY BETTER OFF FOR THE RIFT.

YOU'VE GOT NO RIGHT TO DO THAT! THAT'S MY TREE!!!

SCRUNCH

SOME OF THE VILLAGERS, HAVING OPTED FOR NEUTRALITY, FIND THAT IT HAS ITS DISADVANTAGES.

DINNER'S READY!

COMING, DARLING!

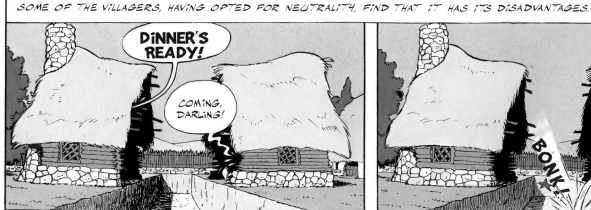

BONK!

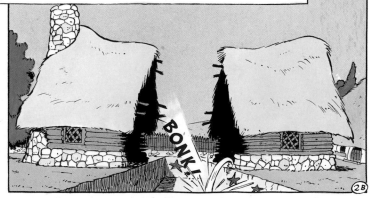

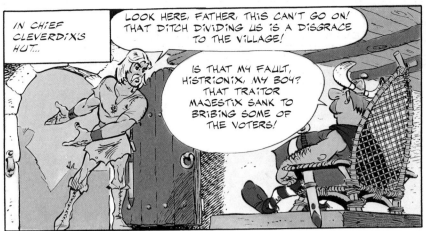

IN CHIEF CLEVERDIX'S HUT...

LOOK HERE, FATHER, THIS CAN'T GO ON! THAT DITCH DIVIDING US IS A DISGRACE TO THE VILLAGE!

IS THAT MY FAULT, HISTRIONIX, MY BOY? THAT TRAITOR MAJESTIX SANK TO BRIBING SOME OF THE VOTERS!

HE AND HIS HENCHMAN, THE UNSPEAKABLE CODFIX, HAD THE NERVE TO GET VOTES FROM VILLAGERS WHO WERE ONLY BABES IN ARMS!

WELL, AT THIS RATE FUTURE GENERATIONS OF GAULS AREN'T GOING TO THINK MUCH OF THEIR ANCESTORS!

CAN YOU SUGGEST ANYTHING, FATHER?

YES, MY BOY, I CAN. I'VE DECIDED TO MAKE A SPEECH TO THE VILLAGERS OPPOSITE. THAT'LL BRIDGE THE GAP. THEY'LL SOON SEE HOW WRONG THEY WERE TO DITCH ME!

AND IN CHIEF MAJESTIX'S HUT...

OH, FATHER, DO YOU REMEMBER HOW HAPPY THE VILLAGE WAS WHEN WE ONLY HAD ONE CHIEF, ALTRUISTIX?

YES, I DO! THE OLD SO-AND-SO TOOK AFTER HIS COUSIN ALCAPONIX... MAKING OFF WITH ALL THE VILLAGE'S TAXES!

THIS IS ALL THAT FOOL CLEVERDIX'S FAULT! HE STOLE VOTES WHICH WERE MINE BY RIGHT.

HE EVEN PROMISED TO BRING DOWN INFLATION, AND THOSE IDIOTS FELL FOR IT! THAT WAS WHEN THE BALLOON WENT UP!

MELODRAMA IS RIGHT! WE NEED A SINGLE CHIEF TO LEAD THE VILLAGE. YOU LET THEM KNOW OVER ON THE LEFT THAT YOU'RE THE RIGHTFUL CHIEF!

CODFIX, YOUR ADVICE ISN'T ALWAYS CODSWALLOP! YES, I'LL ADDRESS THEM!

AND SOON AFTERWARDS...

7

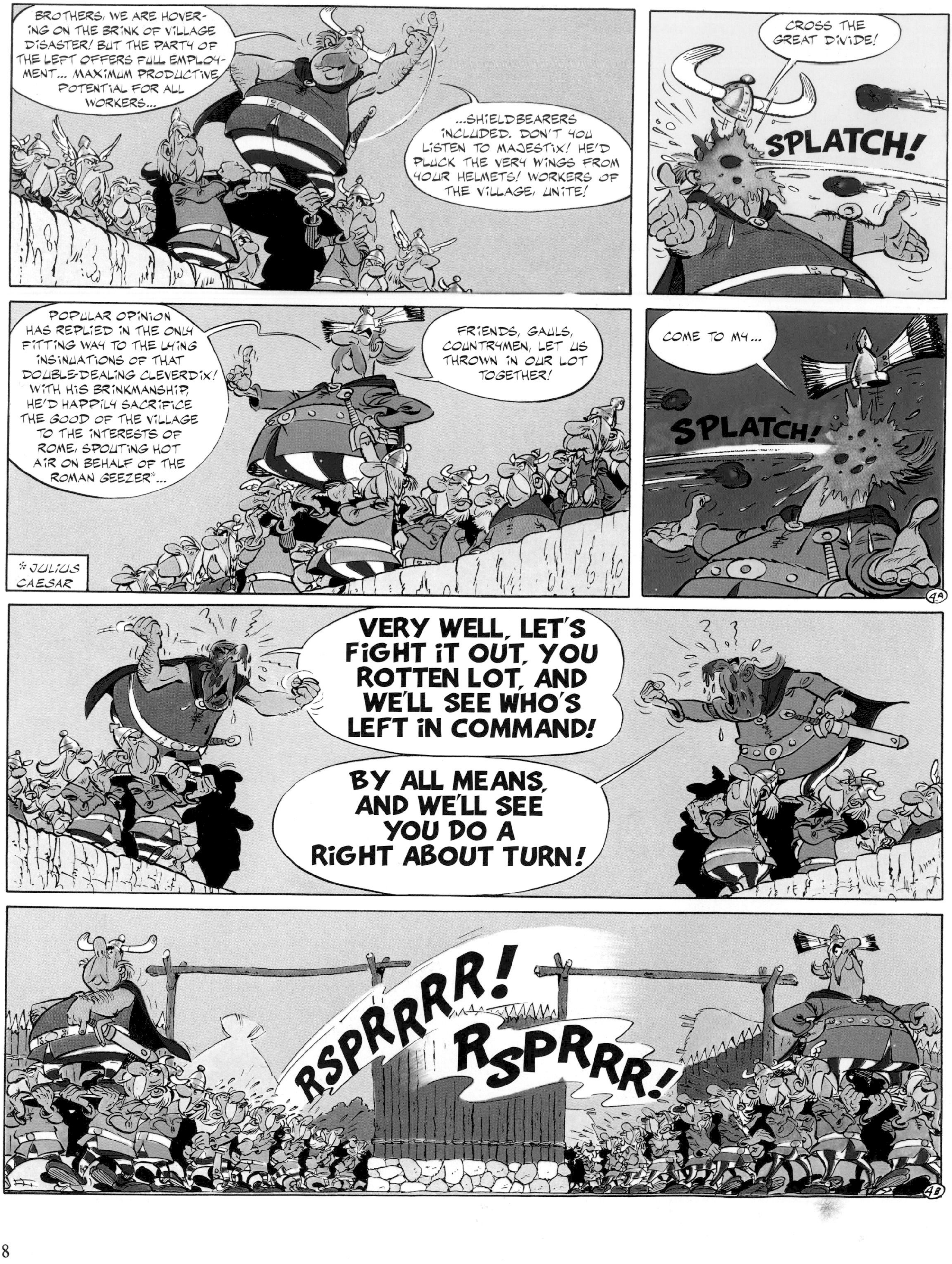

BROTHERS, WE ARE HOVERING ON THE BRINK OF VILLAGE DISASTER! BUT THE PARTY OF THE LEFT OFFERS FULL EMPLOYMENT... MAXIMUM PRODUCTIVE POTENTIAL FOR ALL WORKERS...
...SHIELDBEARERS INCLUDED. DON'T YOU LISTEN TO MAJESTIX! HE'D PLUCK THE VERY WINGS FROM YOUR HELMETS! WORKERS OF THE VILLAGE, UNITE!
CROSS THE GREAT DIVIDE!
SPLATCH!
POPULAR OPINION HAS REPLIED IN THE ONLY FITTING WAY TO THE LYING INSINUATIONS OF THAT DOUBLE-DEALING CLEVERDIX! WITH HIS BRINKMANSHIP, HE'D HAPPILY SACRIFICE THE GOOD OF THE VILLAGE TO THE INTERESTS OF ROME, SPOUTING HOT AIR ON BEHALF OF THE ROMAN GEEZER*...
FRIENDS, GAULS, COUNTRYMEN, LET US THROWN IN OUR LOT TOGETHER!
* JULIUS CAESAR
COME TO MY...
SPLATCH!
4A
VERY WELL, LET'S FIGHT IT OUT, YOU ROTTEN LOT, AND WE'LL SEE WHO'S LEFT IN COMMAND!
BY ALL MEANS, AND WE'LL SEE YOU DO A RIGHT ABOUT TURN!
RSPRRRR!
RSPRRRR!
4B

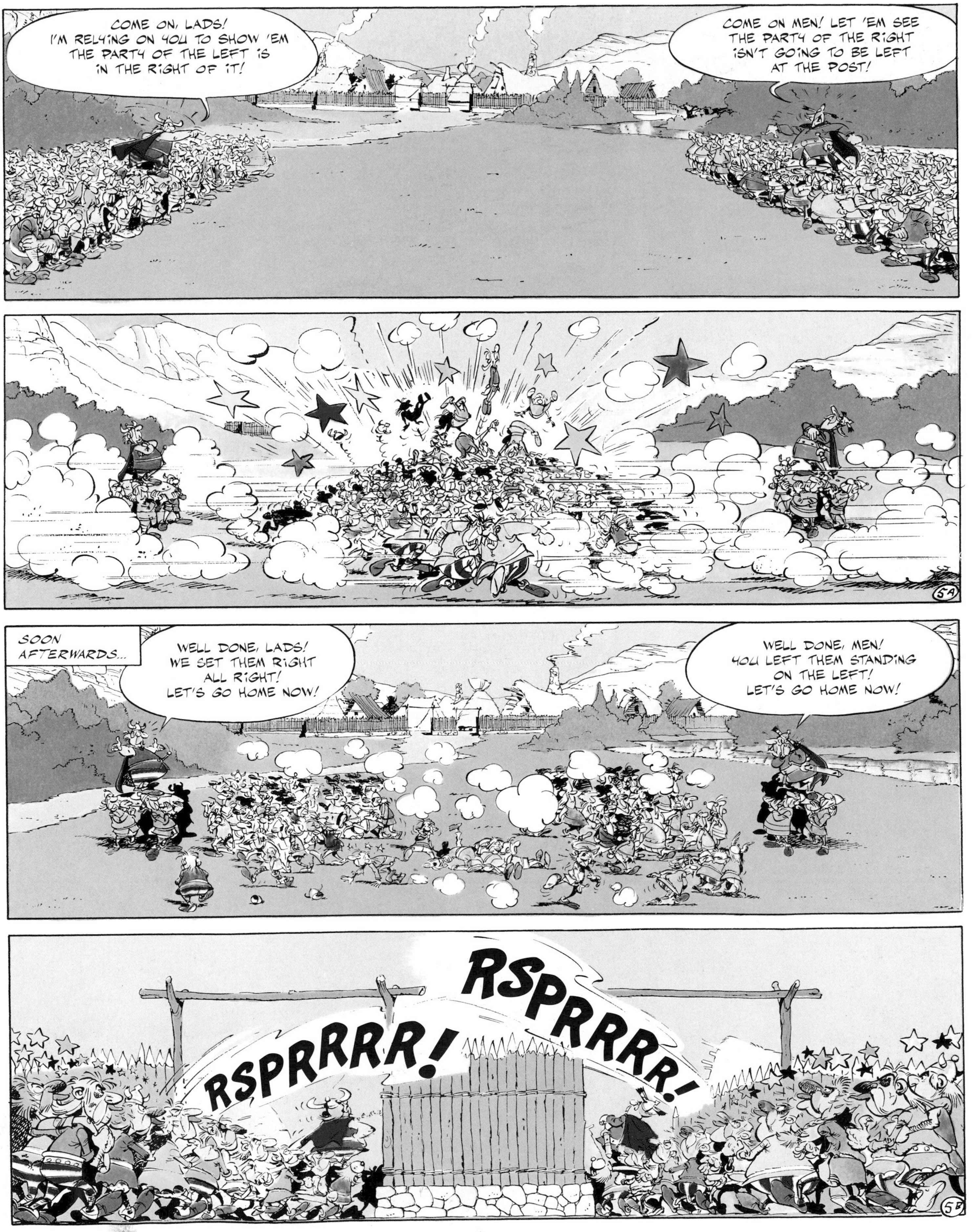
COME ON, LADS! I'M RELYING ON YOU TO SHOW 'EM THE PARTY OF THE LEFT IS IN THE RIGHT OF IT!
COME ON MEN! LET 'EM SEE THE PARTY OF THE RIGHT ISN'T GOING TO BE LEFT AT THE POST!
SOON AFTERWARDS...
WELL DONE, LADS! WE SET THEM RIGHT ALL RIGHT! LET'S GO HOME NOW!
WELL DONE, MEN! YOU LEFT THEM STANDING ON THE LEFT! LET'S GO HOME NOW!
RSPRRRR!
RSPRRRRR!

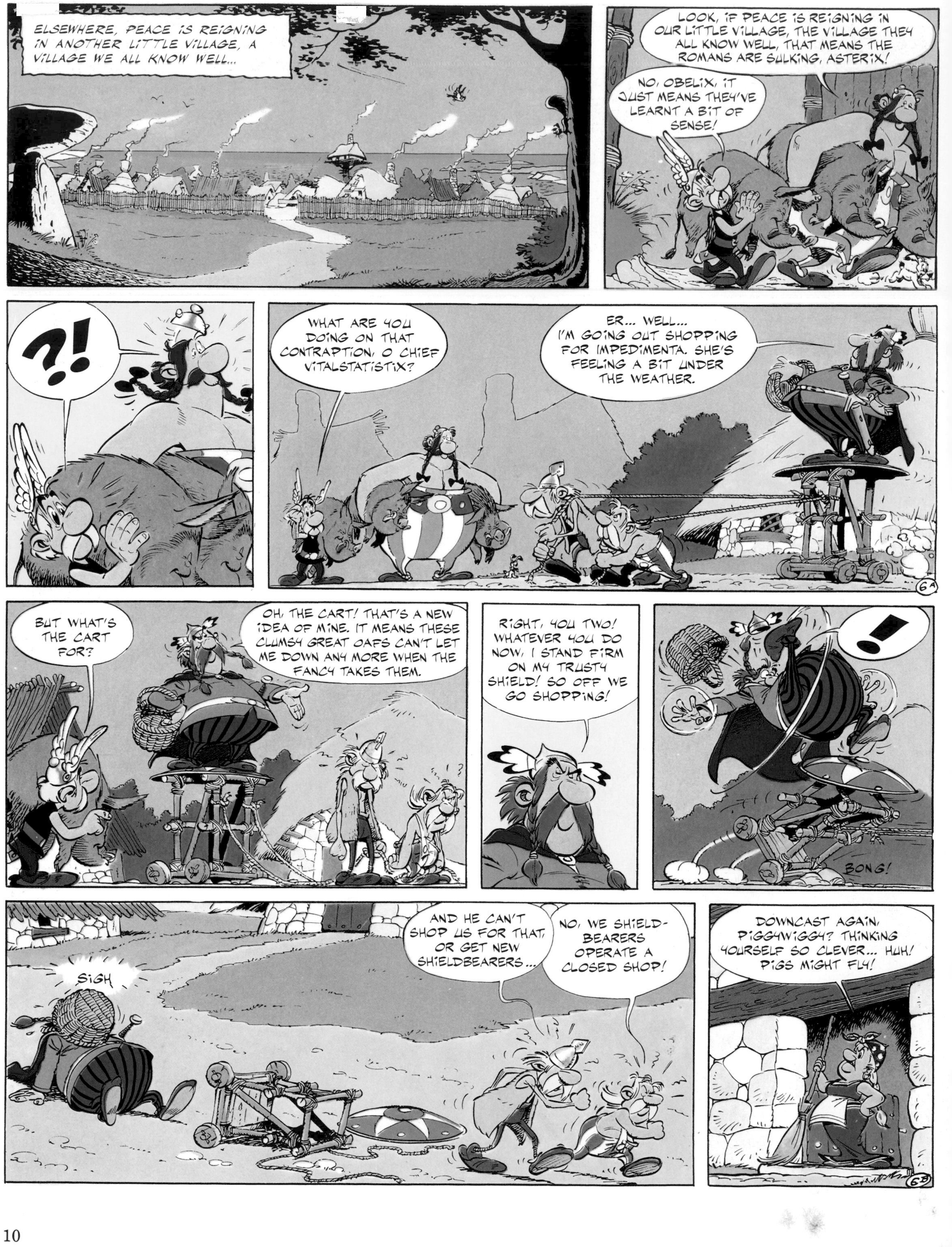
ELSEWHERE, PEACE IS REIGNING IN ANOTHER LITTLE VILLAGE, A VILLAGE WE ALL KNOW WELL...
LOOK, IF PEACE IS REIGNING IN OUR LITTLE VILLAGE, THE VILLAGE THEY ALL KNOW WELL, THAT MEANS THE ROMANS ARE SULKING, ASTERIX!
NO, OBELIX, IT JUST MEANS THEY'VE LEARNT A BIT OF SENSE!
?!
WHAT ARE YOU DOING ON THAT CONTRAPTION, O CHIEF VITALSTATISTIX?
ER... WELL... I'M GOING OUT SHOPPING FOR IMPEDIMENTA. SHE'S FEELING A BIT UNDER THE WEATHER.
BUT WHAT'S THE CART FOR?
OH, THE CART! THAT'S A NEW IDEA OF MINE. IT MEANS THESE CLUMSY GREAT OAFS CAN'T LET ME DOWN ANY MORE WHEN THE FANCY TAKES THEM.
RIGHT, YOU TWO! WHATEVER YOU DO NOW, I STAND FIRM ON MY TRUSTY SHIELD! SO OFF WE GO SHOPPING!
!
BONG!
SIGH
AND HE CAN'T SHOP US FOR THAT, OR GET NEW SHIELDBEARERS...
NO, WE SHIELD-BEARERS OPERATE A CLOSED SHOP!
DOWNCAST AGAIN, PIGGYWIGGY? THINKING YOURSELF SO CLEVER... HUH! PIGS MIGHT FLY!

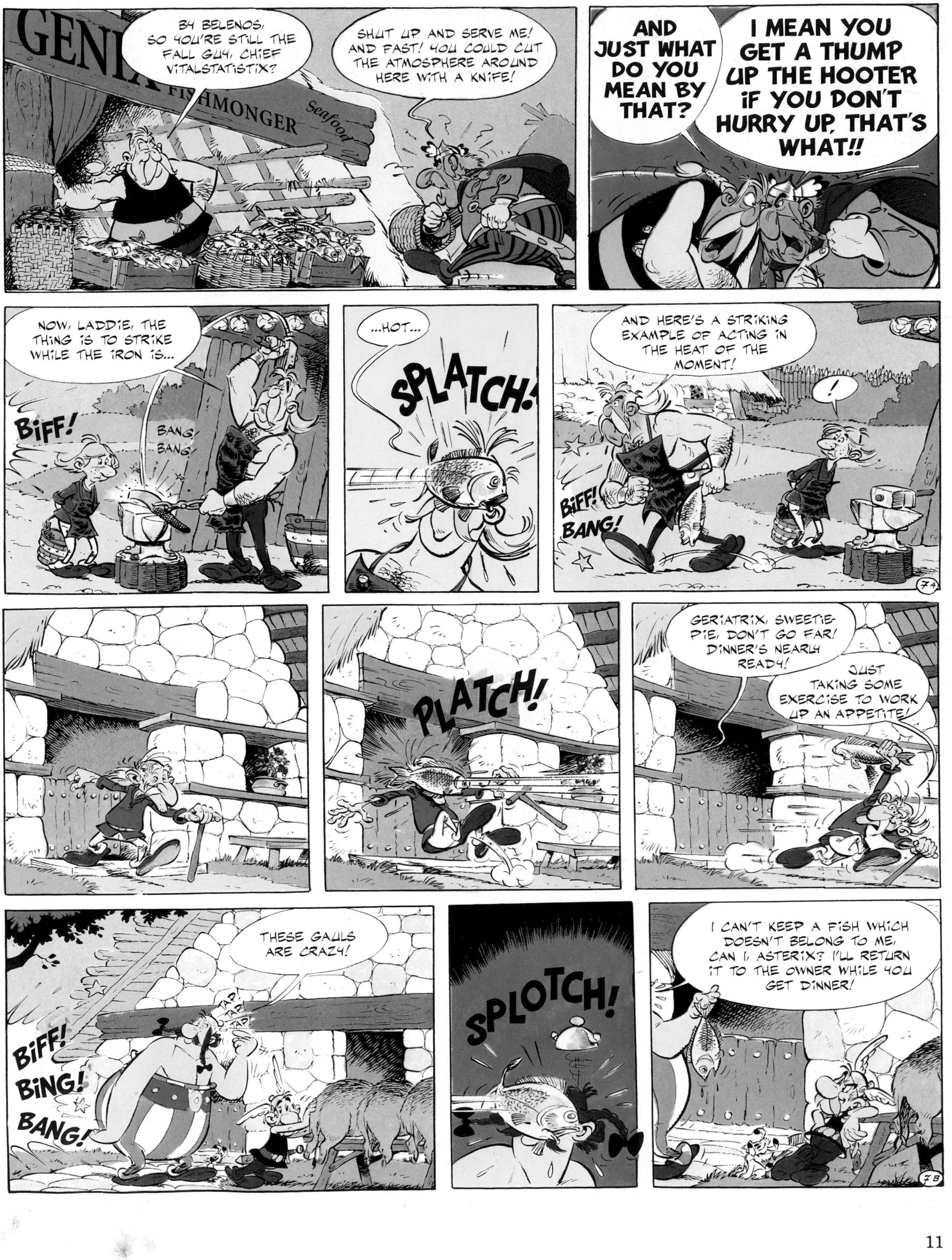
GENIX FISHMONGER Seafood
BY BELENOS, SO YOU'RE STILL THE FALL GUY, CHIEF VITALSTATISTIX?
SHUT UP AND SERVE ME! AND FAST! YOU COULD CUT THE ATMOSPHERE AROUND HERE WITH A KNIFE!
AND JUST WHAT DO YOU MEAN BY THAT?
I MEAN YOU GET A THUMP UP THE HOOTER IF YOU DON'T HURRY UP, THAT'S WHAT!!
NOW, LADDIE, THE THING IS TO STRIKE WHILE THE IRON IS...
BIFF!
BANG! BANG!
...HOT...
SPLATCH!
AND HERE'S A STRIKING EXAMPLE OF ACTING IN THE HEAT OF THE MOMENT!
!
BIFF! BANG!
7A
PLATCH!
GERIATRIX, SWEETIE-PIE, DON'T GO FAR! DINNER'S NEARLY READY!
JUST TAKING SOME EXERCISE TO WORK UP AN APPETITE!
THESE GAULS ARE CRAZY!
TAP! TAP! TAP!
BIFF! BING! BANG!
SPLOTCH!
I CAN'T KEEP A FISH WHICH DOESN'T BELONG TO ME, CAN I, ASTERIX? I'LL RETURN IT TO THE OWNER WHILE YOU GET DINNER!
7B

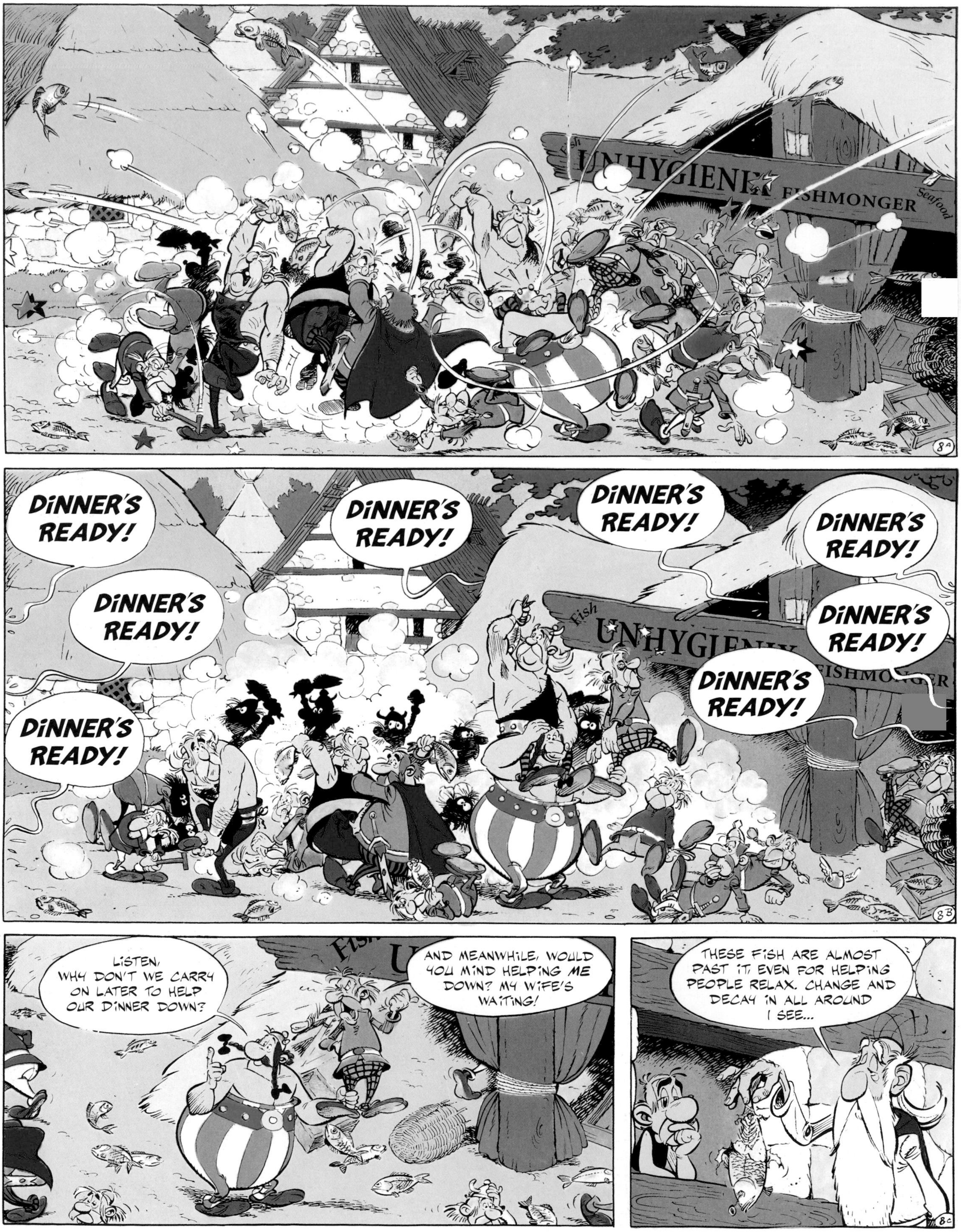
Fish
UNHYGIENI
FISHMONGER
Seafood
DINNER'S READY!
DINNER'S READY!
DINNER'S READY!
DINNER'S READY!
DINNER'S READY!
DINNER'S READY!
DINNER'S READY!
LISTEN, WHY DON'T WE CARRY ON LATER TO HELP OUR DINNER DOWN?
AND MEANWHILE, WOULD YOU MIND HELPING ME DOWN? MY WIFE'S WAITING!
THESE FISH ARE ALMOST PAST IT, EVEN FOR HELPING PEOPLE RELAX. CHANGE AND DECAY IN ALL AROUND I SEE...

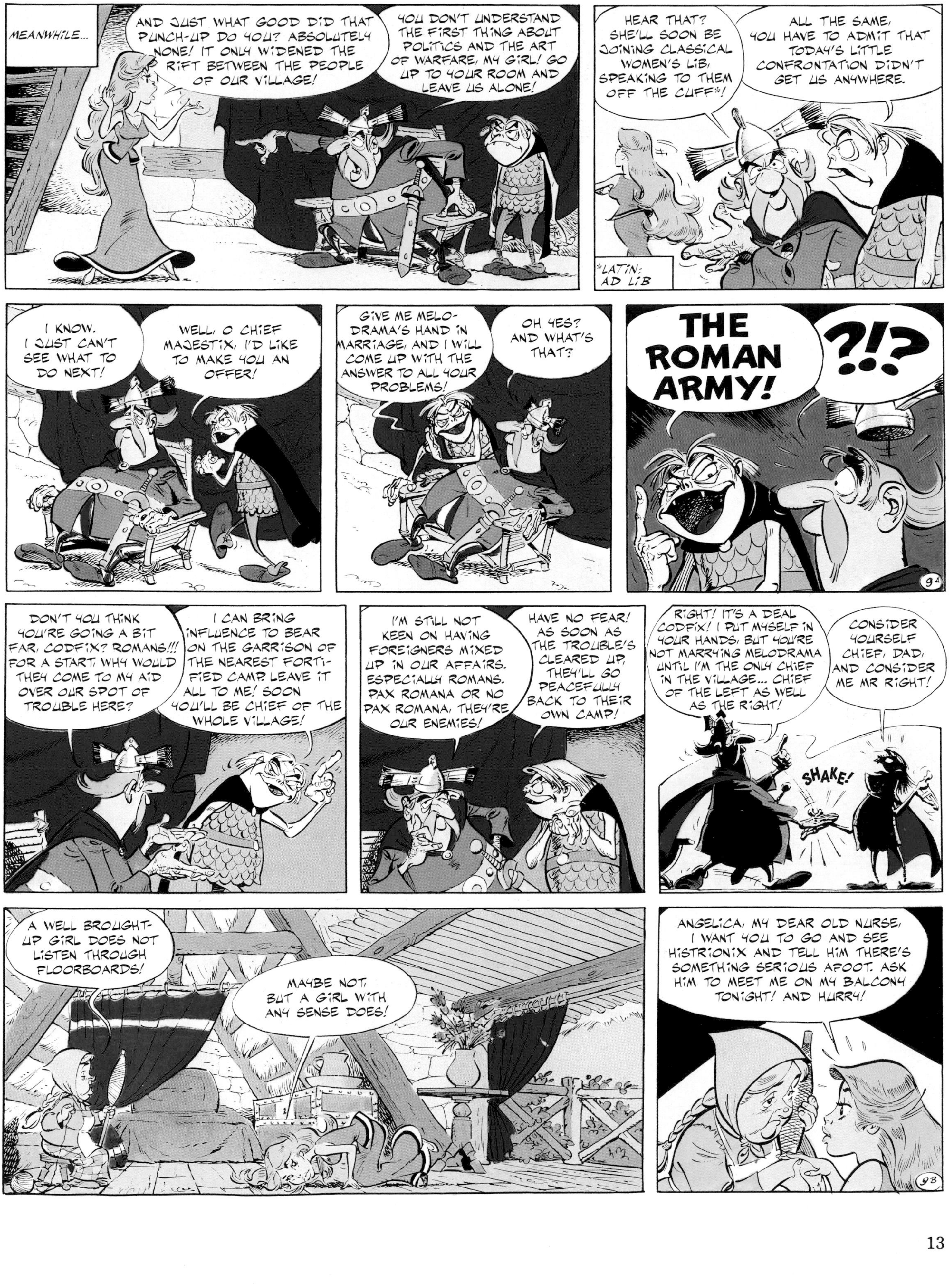
MEANWHILE...
AND JUST WHAT GOOD DID THAT PUNCH-UP DO YOU? ABSOLUTELY NONE! IT ONLY WIDENED THE RIFT BETWEEN THE PEOPLE OF OUR VILLAGE!
YOU DON'T UNDERSTAND THE FIRST THING ABOUT POLITICS AND THE ART OF WARFARE, MY GIRL! GO UP TO YOUR ROOM AND LEAVE US ALONE!
HEAR THAT? SHE'LL SOON BE JOINING CLASSICAL WOMEN'S LIB, SPEAKING TO THEM OFF THE CUFF*!
ALL THE SAME, YOU HAVE TO ADMIT THAT TODAY'S LITTLE CONFRONTATION DIDN'T GET US ANYWHERE.
*LATIN: AD LIB
I KNOW. I JUST CAN'T SEE WHAT TO DO NEXT!
WELL, O CHIEF MAJESTIX, I'D LIKE TO MAKE YOU AN OFFER!
GIVE ME MELODRAMA'S HAND IN MARRIAGE, AND I WILL COME UP WITH THE ANSWER TO ALL YOUR PROBLEMS!
OH YES? AND WHAT'S THAT?
THE ROMAN ARMY!
?!?
DON'T YOU THINK YOU'RE GOING A BIT FAR, CODFIX? ROMANS!!! FOR A START, WHY WOULD THEY COME TO MY AID OVER OUR SPOT OF TROUBLE HERE?
I CAN BRING INFLUENCE TO BEAR ON THE GARRISON OF THE NEAREST FORTIFIED CAMP. LEAVE IT ALL TO ME! SOON YOU'LL BE CHIEF OF THE WHOLE VILLAGE!
I'M STILL NOT KEEN ON HAVING FOREIGNERS MIXED UP IN OUR AFFAIRS. ESPECIALLY ROMANS. PAX ROMANA OR NO PAX ROMANA, THEY'RE OUR ENEMIES!
HAVE NO FEAR! AS SOON AS THE TROUBLE'S CLEARED UP, THEY'LL GO PEACEFULLY BACK TO THEIR OWN CAMP!
RIGHT! IT'S A DEAL CODFIX! I PUT MYSELF IN YOUR HANDS, BUT YOU'RE NOT MARRYING MELODRAMA UNTIL I'M THE ONLY CHIEF IN THE VILLAGE... CHIEF OF THE LEFT AS WELL AS THE RIGHT!
CONSIDER YOURSELF CHIEF, DAD, AND CONSIDER ME MR RIGHT!
SHAKE!
A WELL BROUGHT-UP GIRL DOES NOT LISTEN THROUGH FLOORBOARDS!
MAYBE NOT, BUT A GIRL WITH ANY SENSE DOES!
ANGELICA, MY DEAR OLD NURSE, I WANT YOU TO GO AND SEE HISTRIONIX AND TELL HIM THERE'S SOMETHING SERIOUS AFOOT. ASK HIM TO MEET ME ON MY BALCONY TONIGHT! AND HURRY!

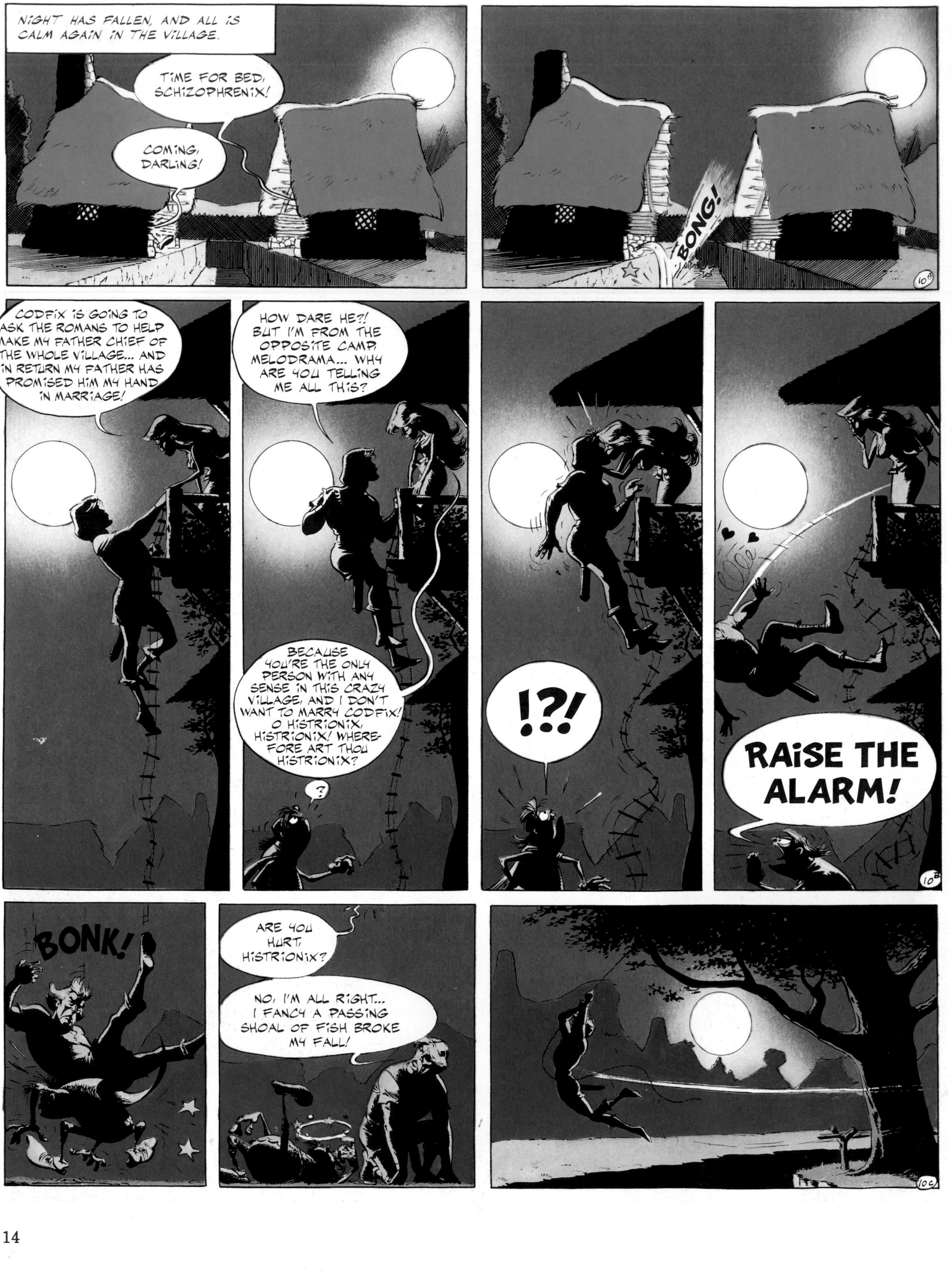
NIGHT HAS FALLEN, AND ALL IS CALM AGAIN IN THE VILLAGE.
TIME FOR BED, SCHIZOPHRENIX!
COMING, DARLING!
BONG!
CODFIX IS GOING TO ASK THE ROMANS TO HELP MAKE MY FATHER CHIEF OF THE WHOLE VILLAGE... AND IN RETURN MY FATHER HAS PROMISED HIM MY HAND IN MARRIAGE!
HOW DARE HE?! BUT I'M FROM THE OPPOSITE CAMP, MELODRAMA... WHY ARE YOU TELLING ME ALL THIS?
BECAUSE YOU'RE THE ONLY PERSON WITH ANY SENSE IN THIS CRAZY VILLAGE, AND I DON'T WANT TO MARRY CODFIX! O HISTRIONIX, HISTRIONIX! WHEREFORE ART THOU HISTRIONIX?
?
!?!
RAISE THE ALARM!
BONK!
ARE YOU HURT, HISTRIONIX?
NO, I'M ALL RIGHT... I FANCY A PASSING SHOAL OF FISH BROKE MY FALL!

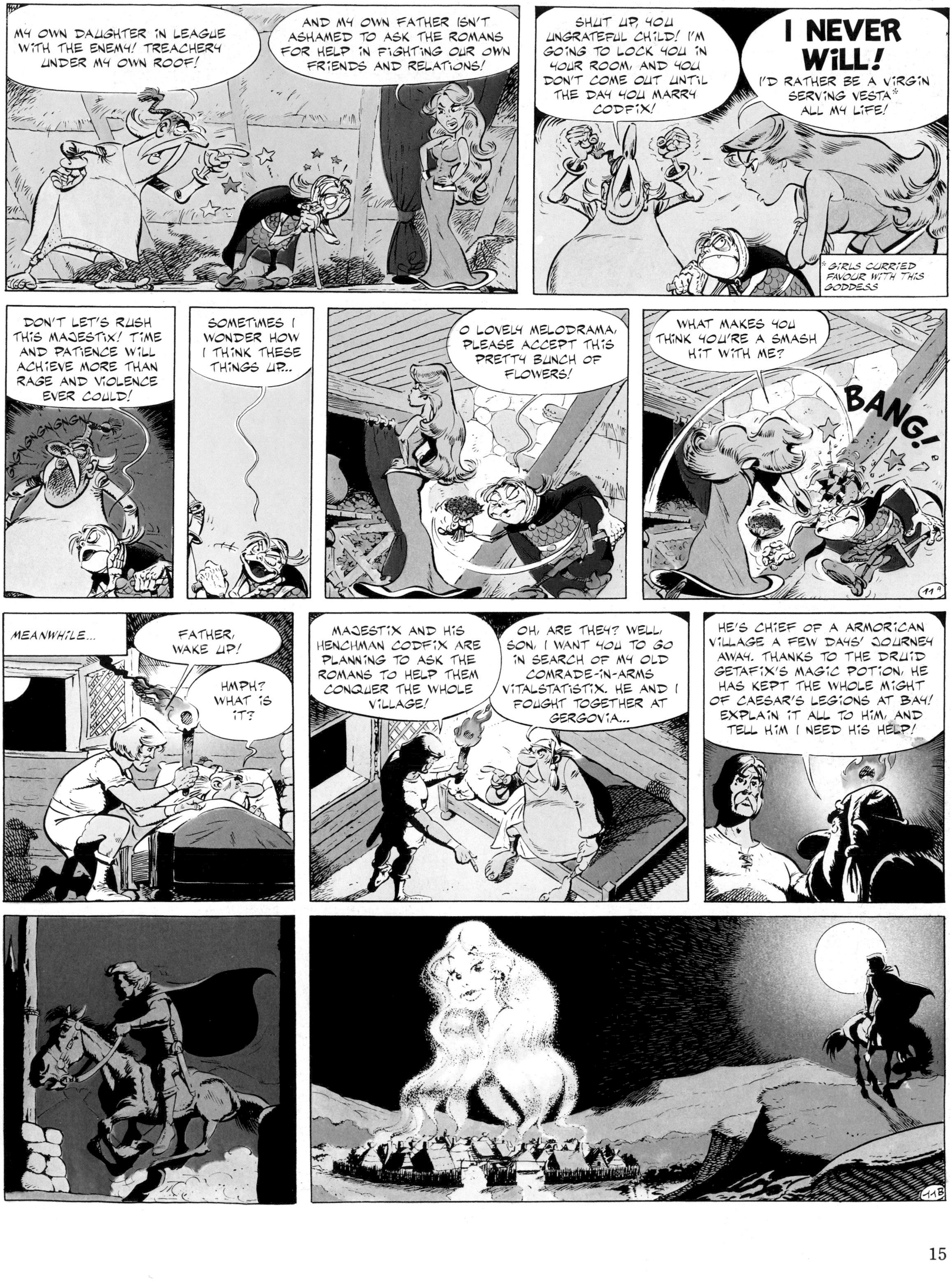
MY OWN DAUGHTER IN LEAGUE WITH THE ENEMY! TREACHERY UNDER MY OWN ROOF!
AND MY OWN FATHER ISN'T ASHAMED TO ASK THE ROMANS FOR HELP IN FIGHTING OUR OWN FRIENDS AND RELATIONS!
SHUT UP, YOU UNGRATEFUL CHILD! I'M GOING TO LOCK YOU IN YOUR ROOM, AND YOU DON'T COME OUT UNTIL THE DAY YOU MARRY CODFIX!
I NEVER WILL! I'D RATHER BE A VIRGIN SERVING VESTA* ALL MY LIFE!
* GIRLS CURRIED FAVOUR WITH THIS GODDESS
DON'T LET'S RUSH THIS MAJESTIX! TIME AND PATIENCE WILL ACHIEVE MORE THAN RAGE AND VIOLENCE EVER COULD!
GNGNGNGNGNGN!
SOMETIMES I WONDER HOW I THINK THESE THINGS UP...
O LOVELY MELODRAMA, PLEASE ACCEPT THIS PRETTY BUNCH OF FLOWERS!
WHAT MAKES YOU THINK YOU'RE A SMASH HIT WITH ME?
BANG!
MEANWHILE...
FATHER, WAKE UP!
HMPH? WHAT IS IT?
MAJESTIX AND HIS HENCHMAN CODFIX ARE PLANNING TO ASK THE ROMANS TO HELP THEM CONQUER THE WHOLE VILLAGE!
OH, ARE THEY? WELL, SON, I WANT YOU TO GO IN SEARCH OF MY OLD COMRADE-IN-ARMS VITALSTATISTIX. HE AND I FOUGHT TOGETHER AT GERGOVIA...
HE'S CHIEF OF A ARMORICAN VILLAGE A FEW DAYS' JOURNEY AWAY. THANKS TO THE DRUID GETAFIX'S MAGIC POTION, HE HAS KEPT THE WHOLE MIGHT OF CAESAR'S LEGIONS AT BAY! EXPLAIN IT ALL TO HIM, AND TELL HIM I NEED HIS HELP!

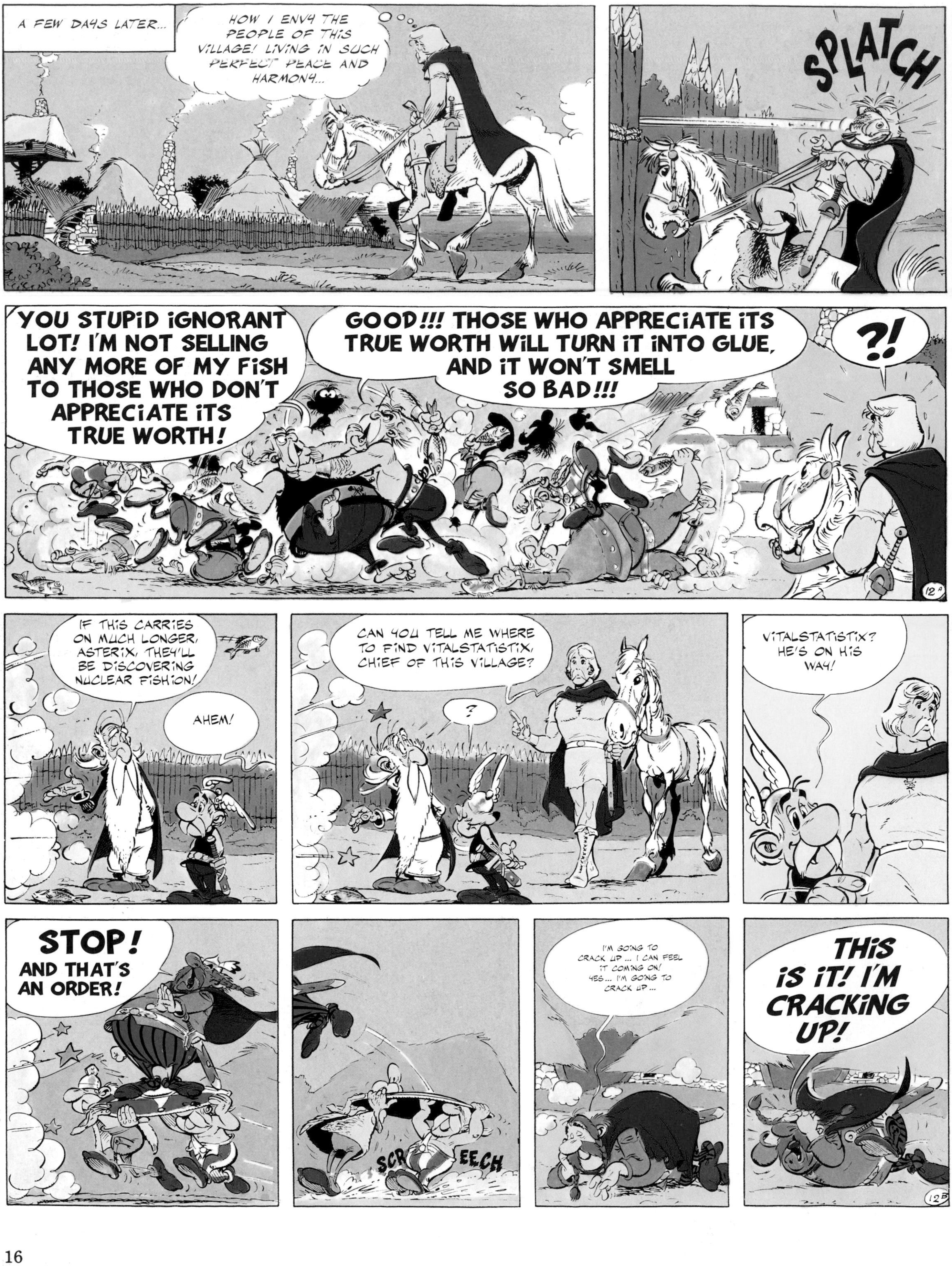
A FEW DAYS LATER...
HOW I ENVY THE PEOPLE OF THIS VILLAGE! LIVING IN SUCH PERFECT PEACE AND HARMONY...
SPLATCH
YOU STUPID IGNORANT LOT! I'M NOT SELLING ANY MORE OF MY FISH TO THOSE WHO DON'T APPRECIATE ITS TRUE WORTH!
GOOD!!! THOSE WHO APPRECIATE ITS TRUE WORTH WILL TURN IT INTO GLUE, AND IT WON'T SMELL SO BAD!!!
?!
IF THIS CARRIES ON MUCH LONGER, ASTERIX, THEY'LL BE DISCOVERING NUCLEAR FISHION!
AHEM!
CAN YOU TELL ME WHERE TO FIND VITALSTATISTIX, CHIEF OF THIS VILLAGE?
?
VITALSTATISTIX? HE'S ON HIS WAY!
STOP! AND THAT'S AN ORDER!
SCR EECH
I'M GOING TO CRACK UP ... I CAN FEEL IT COMING ON! YES... I'M GOING TO CRACK UP ...
THIS IS IT! I'M CRACKING UP!

...AND THAT, O CHIEF VITALSTATISTIX, IS THE SAD STORY OF OUR VILLAGE. ONLY YOUR DRUID GETAFIX'S MAGIC POTION AND THE WISDOM OF YOUR EXPERIENCED WARRIORS CAN SAVE US!

HMPH, YES. SPEAKING OF THE WISDOM OF MY EXPERIENCED WARRIORS, I SOMEHOW FEEL I SHOULD BE PUTTING MY OWN HOUSE IN ORDER FIRST...

...BUT SINCE THE ROMANS LOOK LIKE GETTING MIXED UP IN YOUR AFFAIRS, I DON'T SEE WHY I SHOULDN'T LEND MY OLD COMRADE-IN-ARMS CLEVERDIX A HAND!

THANK YOU... AND ON MY OWN BEHALF TOO! UNLESS WE FIND A PEACEFUL SOLUTION, MELODRAMA AND I CAN NEVER HOPE TO BE UNITED!

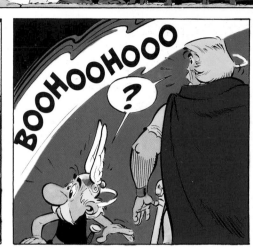

BOOHOOHOOO

?

BOOHOOHOOHOO

WHAT'S THE MATTER, OBELIX?

SNIFF! I GET ALL UPSET BY LOVE STORIES WITH UNHAPPY ENDINGS! SNIFF!

HUH!

BUT THIS STORY'S ONLY JUST BEGINNING, AND IF CHIEF VITALSTATISTIX WILL LET US, WE'RE GOING TO HELP HISTRIONIX SOLVE HIS PROBLEMS!

OOH, YES, LET'S! GOODY, GOODY, GOODY!

WOOF! WOOF!

THE ROMANS AROUND HERE ARE KEEPING VERY QUIET JUST NOW, SO I THINK I CAN JOIN THE EXPEDITION MYSELF! THE PEOPLE OF YOUR VILLAGE MAY NEED ME TO HELP THEM BRIDGE THE GREAT DIVIDE!

AND A LITTLE LATER...

WILL HE SING? WON'T HE SING? WILL HE SING? WON'T HE SING?

17

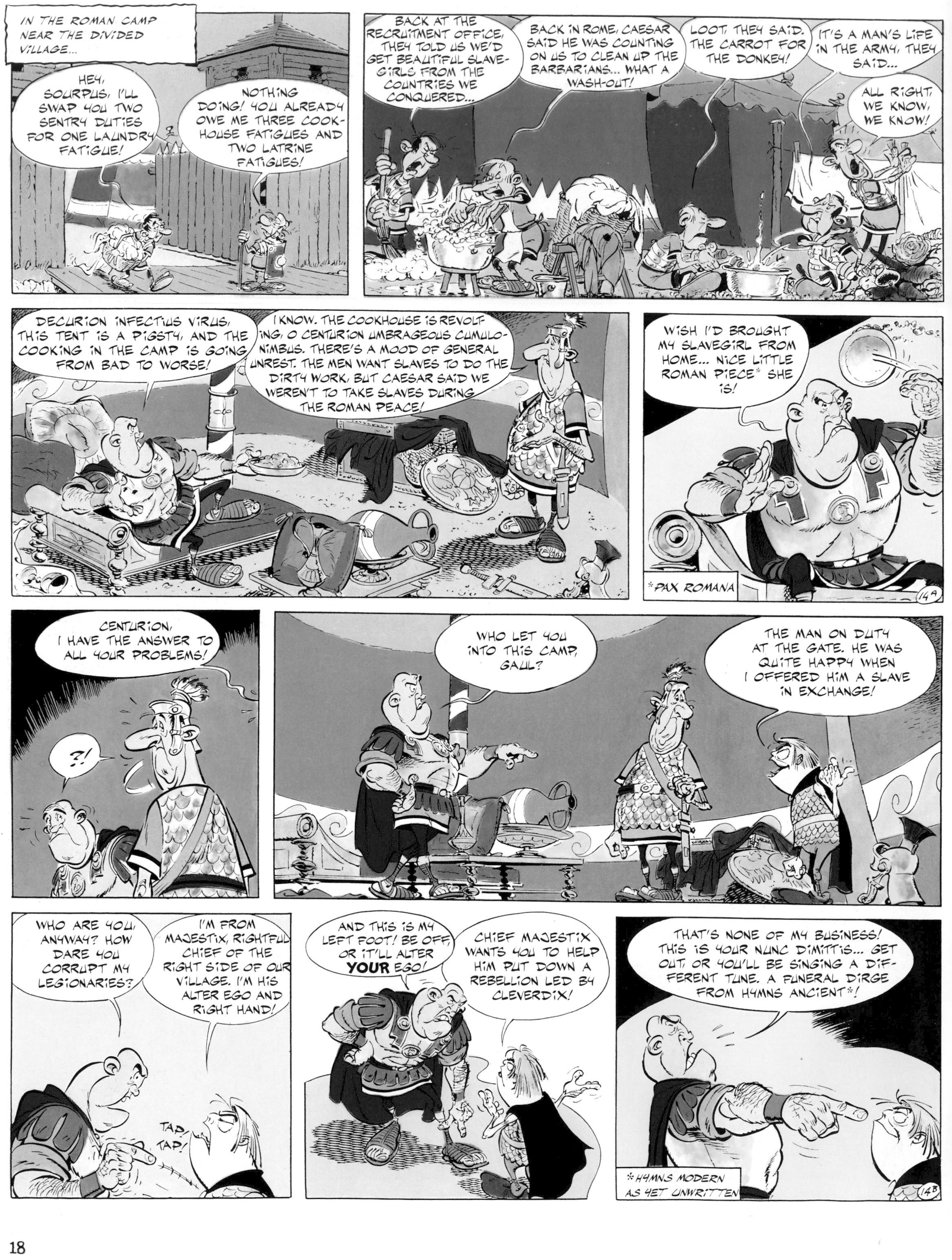

IN THE ROMAN CAMP NEAR THE DIVIDED VILLAGE...
HEY, SOURPUS, I'LL SWAP YOU TWO SENTRY DUTIES FOR ONE LAUNDRY FATIGUE!
NOTHING DOING! YOU ALREADY OWE ME THREE COOK-HOUSE FATIGUES AND TWO LATRINE FATIGUES!
BACK AT THE RECRUITMENT OFFICE, THEY TOLD US WE'D GET BEAUTIFUL SLAVE-GIRLS FROM THE COUNTRIES WE CONQUERED...
BACK IN ROME, CAESAR SAID HE WAS COUNTING ON US TO CLEAN UP THE BARBARIANS... WHAT A WASH-OUT!
LOOT, THEY SAID. THE CARROT FOR THE DONKEY!
IT'S A MAN'S LIFE IN THE ARMY, THEY SAID...
ALL RIGHT, WE KNOW, WE KNOW!
DECURION INFECTIUS VIRUS, THIS TENT IS A PIGSTY, AND THE COOKING IN THE CAMP IS GOING FROM BAD TO WORSE!
I KNOW. THE COOKHOUSE IS REVOLTING, O CENTURION UMBRAGEOUS CUMULONIMBUS. THERE'S A MOOD OF GENERAL UNREST. THE MEN WANT SLAVES TO DO THE DIRTY WORK, BUT CAESAR SAID WE WEREN'T TO TAKE SLAVES DURING THE ROMAN PEACE!
WISH I'D BROUGHT MY SLAVEGIRL FROM HOME... NICE LITTLE ROMAN PIECE* SHE IS!
*PAX ROMANA
14A
CENTURION, I HAVE THE ANSWER TO ALL YOUR PROBLEMS!
?!
WHO LET YOU INTO THIS CAMP, GAUL?
THE MAN ON DUTY AT THE GATE. HE WAS QUITE HAPPY WHEN I OFFERED HIM A SLAVE IN EXCHANGE!
WHO ARE YOU, ANYWAY? HOW DARE YOU CORRUPT MY LEGIONARIES?
I'M FROM MAJESTIX, RIGHTFUL CHIEF OF THE RIGHT SIDE OF OUR VILLAGE. I'M HIS ALTER EGO AND RIGHT HAND!
TAP, TAP!
AND THIS IS MY LEFT FOOT! BE OFF, OR IT'LL ALTER YOUR EGO!
CHIEF MAJESTIX WANTS YOU TO HELP HIM PUT DOWN A REBELLION LED BY CLEVERDIX!
THAT'S NONE OF MY BUSINESS! THIS IS YOUR NUNC DIMITTIS... GET OUT, OR YOU'LL BE SINGING A DIFFERENT TUNE. A FUNERAL DIRGE FROM HYMNS ANCIENT*!
*HYMNS MODERN AS YET UNWRITTEN
14B

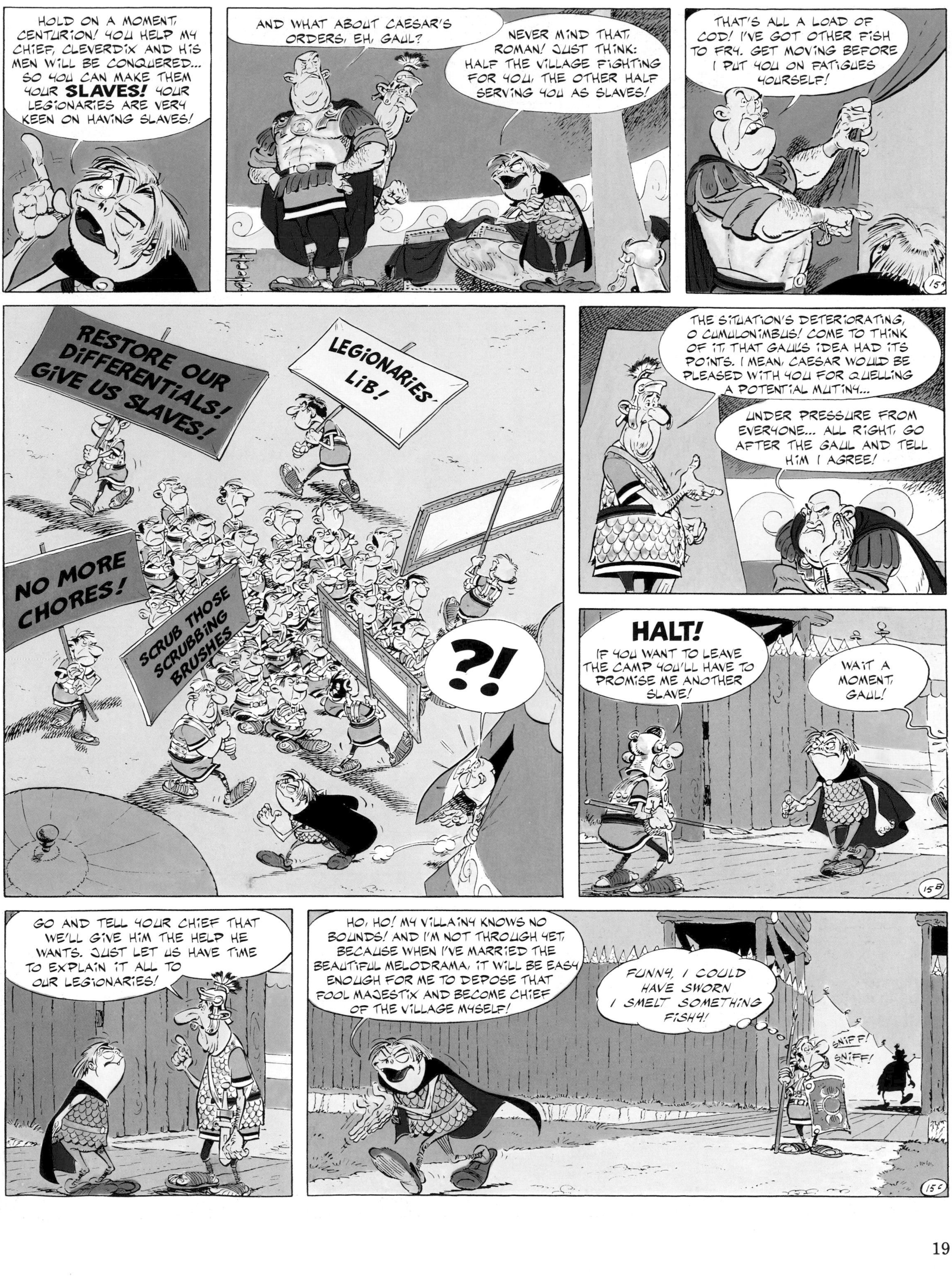
HOLD ON A MOMENT, CENTURION! YOU HELP MY CHIEF, CLEVERDIX AND HIS MEN WILL BE CONQUERED... SO YOU CAN MAKE THEM YOUR **SLAVES!** YOUR LEGIONARIES ARE VERY KEEN ON HAVING SLAVES!
AND WHAT ABOUT CAESAR'S ORDERS, EH, GAUL?
NEVER MIND THAT, ROMAN! JUST THINK: HALF THE VILLAGE FIGHTING FOR YOU, THE OTHER HALF SERVING YOU AS SLAVES!
THAT'S ALL A LOAD OF COD! I'VE GOT OTHER FISH TO FRY. GET MOVING BEFORE I PUT YOU ON FATIGUES YOURSELF!
15A
RESTORE OUR DIFFERENTIALS! GIVE US SLAVES!
LEGIONARIES' LIB!
NO MORE CHORES!
SCRUB THOSE SCRUBBING BRUSHES
?!
THE SITUATION'S DETERIORATING, O CUMULONIMBUS! COME TO THINK OF IT, THAT GAUL'S IDEA HAD ITS POINTS. I MEAN, CAESAR WOULD BE PLEASED WITH YOU FOR QUELLING A POTENTIAL MUTINY...
UNDER PRESSURE FROM EVERYONE... ALL RIGHT, GO AFTER THE GAUL AND TELL HIM I AGREE!
HALT! IF YOU WANT TO LEAVE THE CAMP YOU'LL HAVE TO PROMISE ME ANOTHER SLAVE!
WAIT A MOMENT, GAUL!
15B
GO AND TELL YOUR CHIEF THAT WE'LL GIVE HIM THE HELP HE WANTS. JUST LET US HAVE TIME TO EXPLAIN IT ALL TO OUR LEGIONARIES!
HO, HO! MY VILLAINY KNOWS NO BOUNDS! AND I'M NOT THROUGH YET, BECAUSE WHEN I'VE MARRIED THE BEAUTIFUL MELODRAMA, IT WILL BE EASY ENOUGH FOR ME TO DEPOSE THAT FOOL MAJESTIX AND BECOME CHIEF OF THE VILLAGE MYSELF!
FUNNY, I COULD HAVE SWORN I SMELT SOMETHING FISHY!
SNIFF! SNIFF!
15C

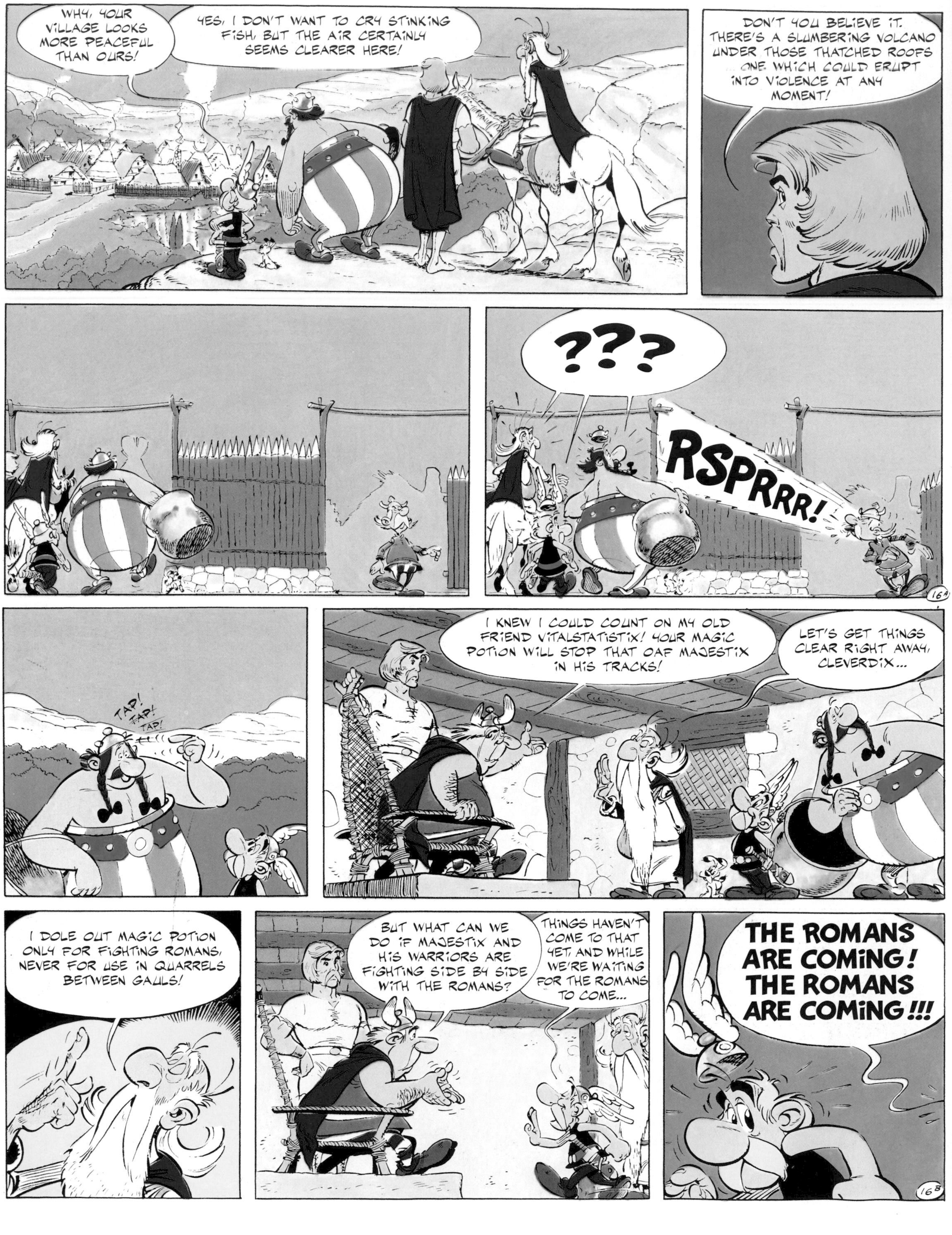

WHY, YOUR VILLAGE LOOKS MORE PEACEFUL THAN OURS!
YES, I DON'T WANT TO CRY STINKING FISH, BUT THE AIR CERTAINLY SEEMS CLEARER HERE!
DON'T YOU BELIEVE IT. THERE'S A SLUMBERING VOLCANO UNDER THOSE THATCHED ROOFS ... ONE WHICH COULD ERUPT INTO VIOLENCE AT ANY MOMENT!
???
RSPRRR!
16A
TAP! TAP! TAP!
I KNEW I COULD COUNT ON MY OLD FRIEND VITALSTATISTIX! YOUR MAGIC POTION WILL STOP THAT OAF MAJESTIX IN HIS TRACKS!
LET'S GET THINGS CLEAR RIGHT AWAY, CLEVERDIX...
I DOLE OUT MAGIC POTION ONLY FOR FIGHTING ROMANS, NEVER FOR USE IN QUARRELS BETWEEN GAULS!
BUT WHAT CAN WE DO IF MAJESTIX AND HIS WARRIORS ARE FIGHTING SIDE BY SIDE WITH THE ROMANS?
THINGS HAVEN'T COME TO THAT YET, AND WHILE WE'RE WAITING FOR THE ROMANS TO COME...
THE ROMANS ARE COMING! THE ROMANS ARE COMING!!!
16B

THE ROMANS ARE ADVANCING TOWARDS THE VILLAGE! YOU CAN GET MELODRAMA'S DOWRY READY, MAJESTIX!

RIGHT! CALL ALL OUR WARRIOR'S TOGETHER! WE WILL GO OUT AND WELCOME THE ROMANS!

AND TELL OUR MEN TO LEAVE THEIR WEAPONS AT HOME. WE MUST SHOW THAT WE COME IN GOOD FAITH!

HURRAH! OFF TO THE SLAVE MARKET! I'M SLAVERING WITH ANTICIPATION!

YEAH! NO MORE FATIGUES FOR US, AND I'M HANDING BACK THOSE THREE SENTRY DUTIES YOU SWAPPED ME FOR ONE COOKHOUSE FATIGUE!

SHALL WE GET THEM, ASTERIX?

WAIT A MOMENT, OBELIX! NOT YET.

SEE THAT, DRUID? WE REALLY DO NEED YOUR MAGIC POTION!

I'M AFRAID IT'S TOO LATE TO MAKE ANY NOW...

WELCOME, O ROMAN! OUR GRATITUDE FOR YOUR VALUABLE ASSISTANCE KNOWS NO BOUNDS, AND...

CUT THE CACKLE! WHERE ARE THE SLAVES?

SLAVES? WHAT SLAVES!!!

THE SLAVES YOUR FISH-FACED FRIEND PROMISED IN THE SMALL PRINT OF THE CONTRACT!

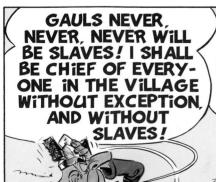

GAULS NEVER, NEVER, NEVER WILL BE SLAVES! I SHALL BE CHIEF OF EVERYONE IN THE VILLAGE WITHOUT EXCEPTION, AND WITHOUT SLAVES!

YOU DON'T GO CALLING OUT THE ROMAN ARMY FOR NOTHING! MEN, GRAB HOLD OF THIS LOT! THEY CAN BE OUR SLAVES THEMSELVES!

HELP! THAT FOOL MAJESTIX HAS RUINED EVERYTHING!

21

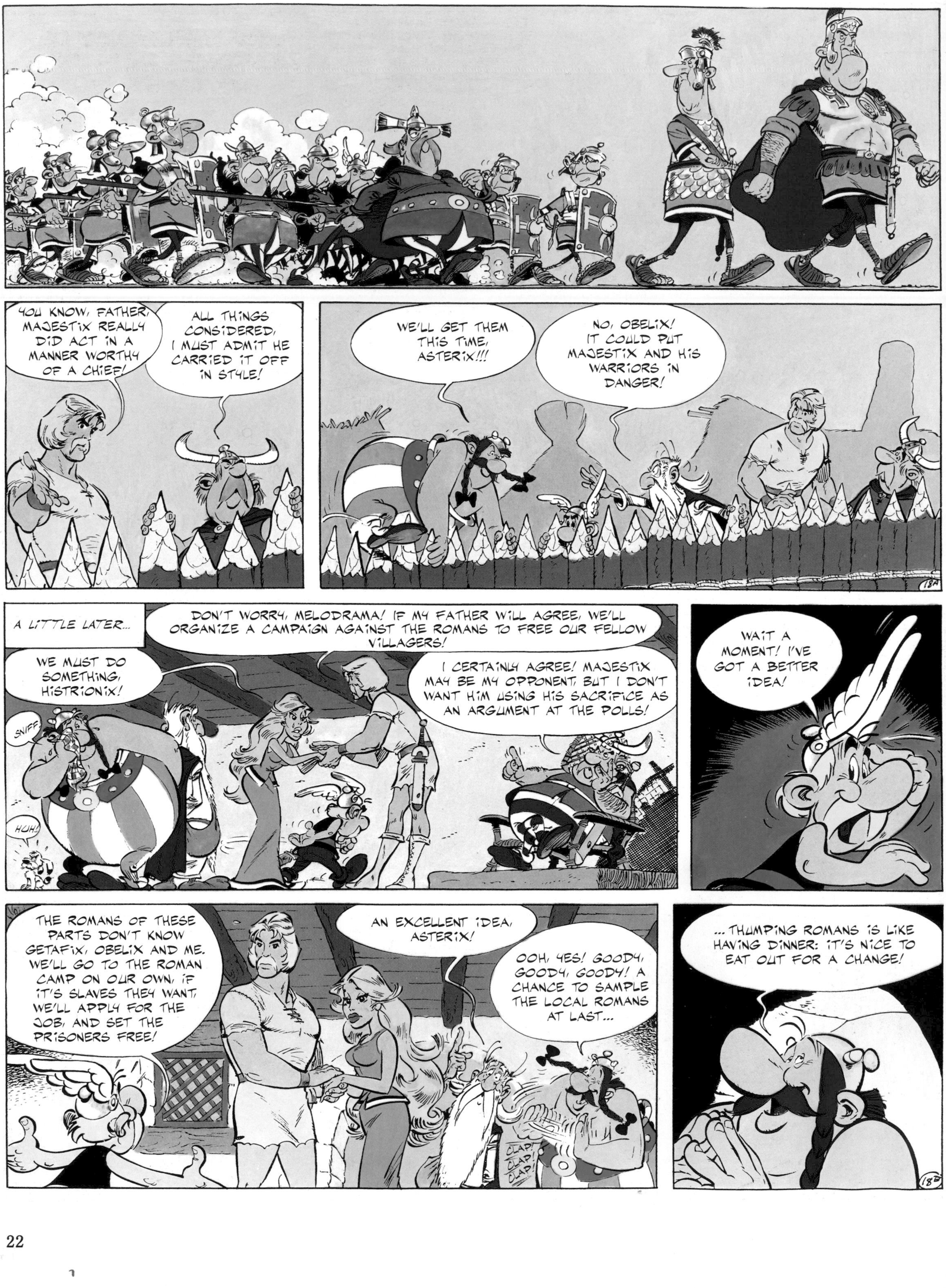
YOU KNOW, FATHER, MAJESTIX REALLY DID ACT IN A MANNER WORTHY OF A CHIEF!
ALL THINGS CONSIDERED, I MUST ADMIT HE CARRIED IT OFF IN STYLE!
WE'LL GET THEM THIS TIME, ASTERIX!!!
NO, OBELIX! IT COULD PUT MAJESTIX AND HIS WARRIORS IN DANGER!
A LITTLE LATER...
DON'T WORRY, MELODRAMA! IF MY FATHER WILL AGREE, WE'LL ORGANIZE A CAMPAIGN AGAINST THE ROMANS TO FREE OUR FELLOW VILLAGERS!
WE MUST DO SOMETHING, HISTRIONIX!
SNIFF
HUH!
I CERTAINLY AGREE! MAJESTIX MAY BE MY OPPONENT, BUT I DON'T WANT HIM USING HIS SACRIFICE AS AN ARGUMENT AT THE POLLS!
WAIT A MOMENT! I'VE GOT A BETTER IDEA!
THE ROMANS OF THESE PARTS DON'T KNOW GETAFIX, OBELIX AND ME. WE'LL GO TO THE ROMAN CAMP ON OUR OWN, IF IT'S SLAVES THEY WANT, WE'LL APPLY FOR THE JOB, AND SET THE PRISONERS FREE!
AN EXCELLENT IDEA, ASTERIX!
OOH, YES! GOODY, GOODY, GOODY! A CHANCE TO SAMPLE THE LOCAL ROMANS AT LAST...
CLAP! CLAP! CLAP!
... THUMPING ROMANS IS LIKE HAVING DINNER: IT'S NICE TO EAT OUT FOR A CHANGE!

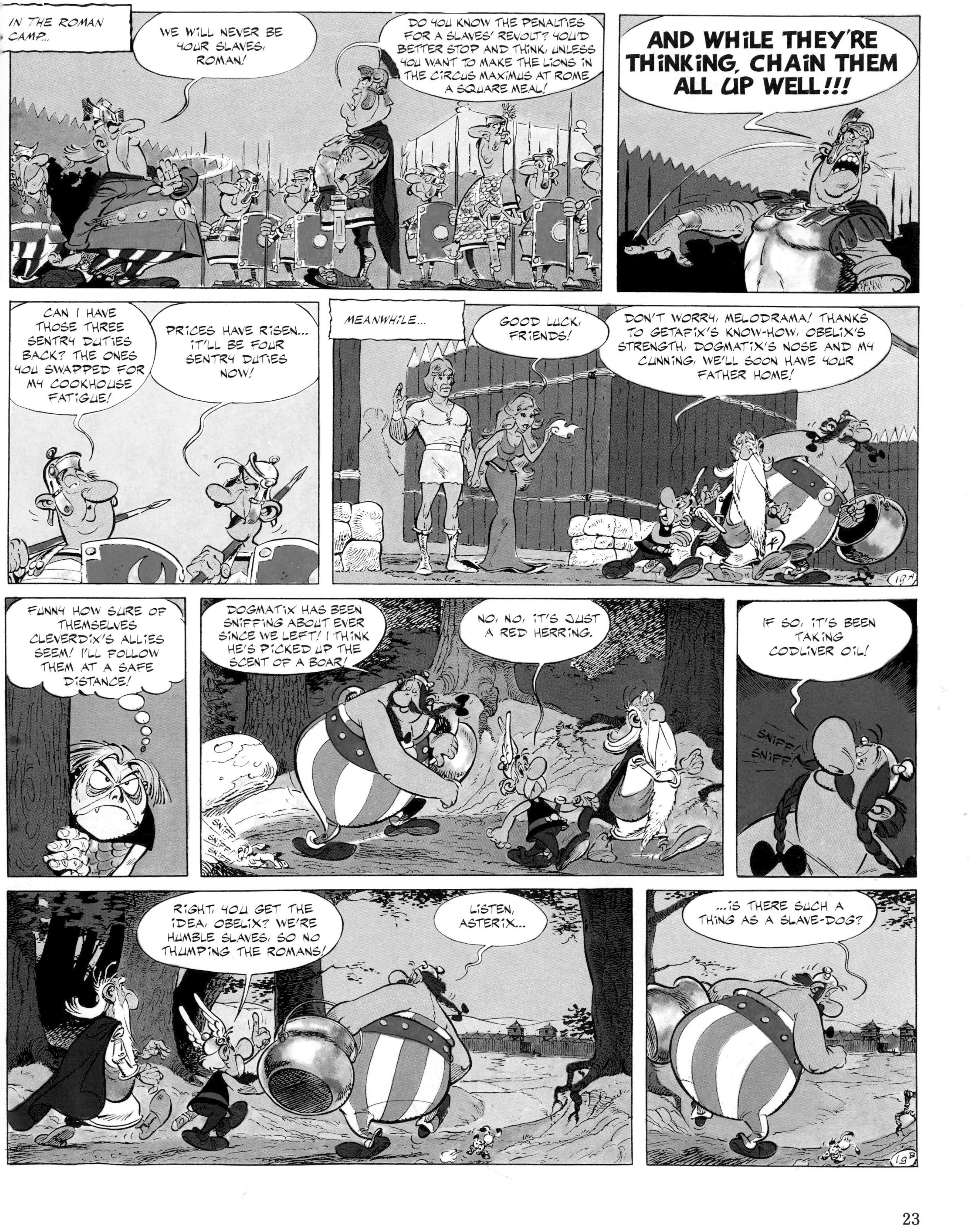

IN THE ROMAN CAMP...
WE WILL NEVER BE YOUR SLAVES, ROMAN!
DO YOU KNOW THE PENALTIES FOR A SLAVES' REVOLT? YOU'D BETTER STOP AND THINK, UNLESS YOU WANT TO MAKE THE LIONS IN THE CIRCUS MAXIMUS AT ROME A SQUARE MEAL!
AND WHILE THEY'RE THINKING, CHAIN THEM ALL UP WELL!!!
CAN I HAVE THOSE THREE SENTRY DUTIES BACK? THE ONES YOU SWAPPED FOR MY COOKHOUSE FATIGUE!
PRICES HAVE RISEN... IT'LL BE FOUR SENTRY DUTIES NOW!
MEANWHILE...
GOOD LUCK, FRIENDS!
DON'T WORRY, MELODRAMA! THANKS TO GETAFIX'S KNOW-HOW, OBELIX'S STRENGTH, DOGMATIX'S NOSE AND MY CUNNING, WE'LL SOON HAVE YOUR FATHER HOME!
FUNNY HOW SURE OF THEMSELVES CLEVERDIX'S ALLIES SEEM! I'LL FOLLOW THEM AT A SAFE DISTANCE!
DOGMATIX HAS BEEN SNIFFING ABOUT EVER SINCE WE LEFT! I THINK HE'S PICKED UP THE SCENT OF A BOAR!
NO, NO, IT'S JUST A RED HERRING.
SNIFF! SNIFF! SNIFF!
IF SO, IT'S BEEN TAKING CODLIVER OIL!
SNIFF! SNIFF!
RIGHT, YOU GET THE IDEA, OBELIX? WE'RE HUMBLE SLAVES, SO NO THUMPING THE ROMANS!
LISTEN, ASTERIX...
...IS THERE SUCH A THING AS A SLAVE-DOG?

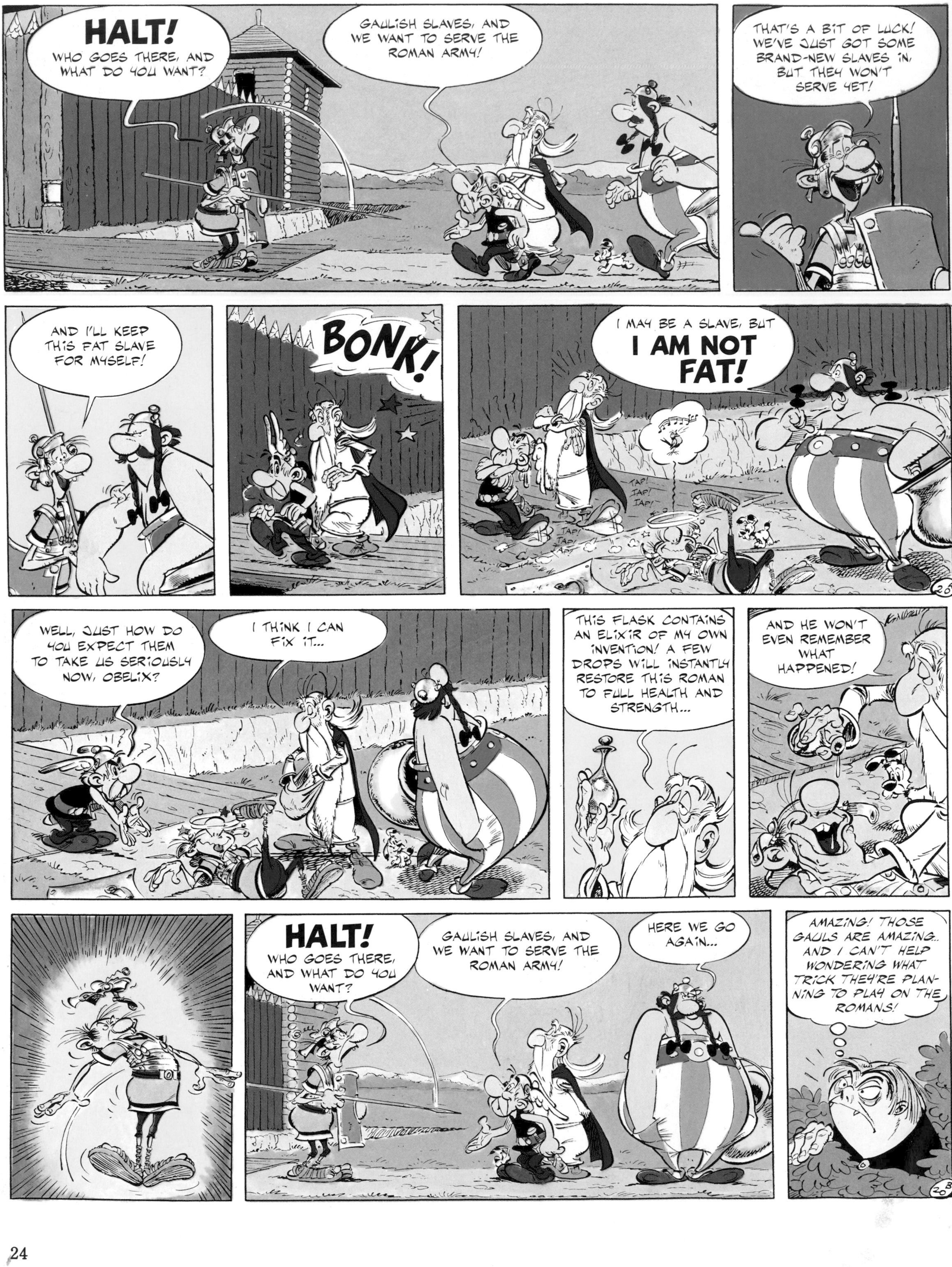

HALT! WHO GOES THERE, AND WHAT DO YOU WANT?
GAULISH SLAVES, AND WE WANT TO SERVE THE ROMAN ARMY!
THAT'S A BIT OF LUCK! WE'VE JUST GOT SOME BRAND-NEW SLAVES IN, BUT THEY WON'T SERVE YET!
AND I'LL KEEP THIS FAT SLAVE FOR MYSELF!
BONK!
I MAY BE A SLAVE, BUT I AM NOT FAT!
TAP! TAP! TAP!
TAP! TAP! TAP!
WELL, JUST HOW DO YOU EXPECT THEM TO TAKE US SERIOUSLY NOW, OBELIX?
I THINK I CAN FIX IT...
THIS FLASK CONTAINS AN ELIXIR OF MY OWN INVENTION! A FEW DROPS WILL INSTANTLY RESTORE THIS ROMAN TO FULL HEALTH AND STRENGTH...
AND HE WON'T EVEN REMEMBER WHAT HAPPENED!
HALT! WHO GOES THERE, AND WHAT DO YOU WANT?
GAULISH SLAVES, AND WE WANT TO SERVE THE ROMAN ARMY!
HERE WE GO AGAIN...
AMAZING! THOSE GAULS ARE AMAZING.. AND I CAN'T HELP WONDERING WHAT TRICK THEY'RE PLANNING TO PLAY ON THE ROMANS!

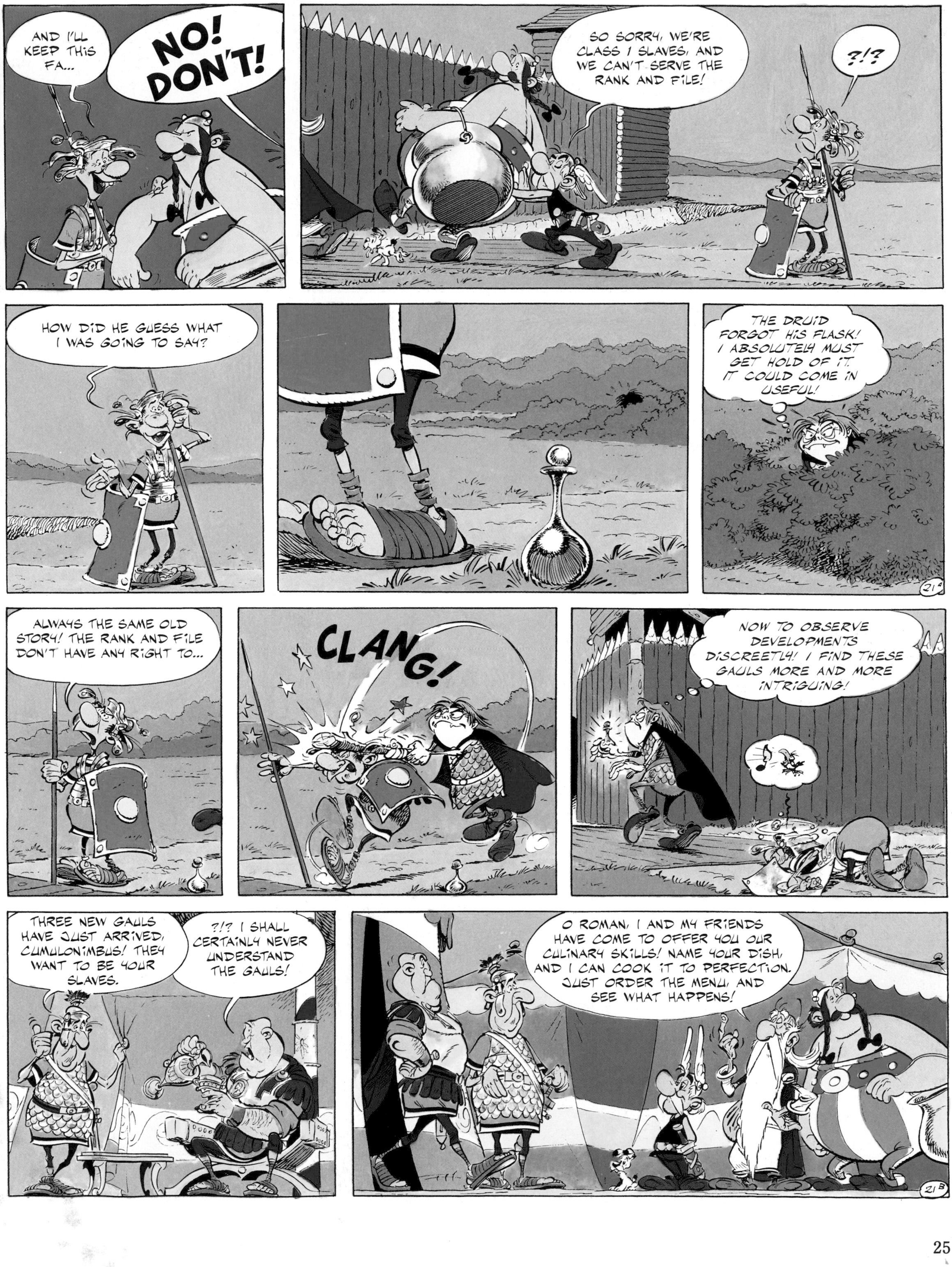
AND I'LL KEEP THIS FA...
NO! DON'T!
SO SORRY, WE'RE CLASS I SLAVES, AND WE CAN'T SERVE THE RANK AND FILE!
?!?
HOW DID HE GUESS WHAT I WAS GOING TO SAY?
THE DRUID FORGOT HIS FLASK! I ABSOLUTELY MUST GET HOLD OF IT. IT COULD COME IN USEFUL!
21A
ALWAYS THE SAME OLD STORY! THE RANK AND FILE DON'T HAVE ANY RIGHT TO...
CLANG!
NOW TO OBSERVE DEVELOPMENTS DISCREETLY! I FIND THESE GAULS MORE AND MORE INTRIGUING!
THREE NEW GAULS HAVE JUST ARRIVED, CUMULONIMBUS! THEY WANT TO BE YOUR SLAVES.
?!? I SHALL CERTAINLY NEVER UNDERSTAND THE GAULS!
O ROMAN, I AND MY FRIENDS HAVE COME TO OFFER YOU OUR CULINARY SKILLS! NAME YOUR DISH, AND I CAN COOK IT TO PERFECTION. JUST ORDER THE MENU, AND SEE WHAT HAPPENS!
21B

THE GODS MUST HAVE SENT YOU, GAUL! A SPOT OF GOOD COOKING WILL CERTAINLY MAKE A CHANGE FROM THE USUAL MESS!

OH, WE CAN COOK A GOOD MEAL FOR ALL YOUR MEN, CENTURION! THE FEAST OF THE CENTURY, AS YOU MIGHT SAY!

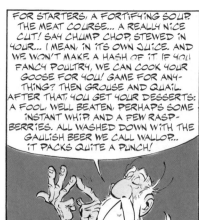

FOR STARTERS, A FORTIFYING SOUP. THE MEAT COURSE... A REALLY NICE CUT! SAY CHUMP CHOP, STEWED IN YOUR... I MEAN, IN ITS OWN JUICE. AND WE WON'T MAKE A HASH OF IT! IF YOU FANCY POULTRY, WE CAN COOK YOUR GOOSE FOR YOU! GAME FOR ANYTHING? THEN GROUSE AND QUAIL. AFTER THAT YOU GET YOUR DESSERTS: A FOOL, WELL BEATEN, PERHAPS SOME INSTANT WHIP AND A FEW RASPBERRIES. ALL WASHED DOWN WITH THE GAULISH BEER WE CALL WALLOP... IT PACKS QUITE A PUNCH!

THAT'LL DO FINE! GET ON WITH IT... I CAN HARDLY WAIT!

WE SHAN'T TAKE LONG!

WINK

LOOK HERE, GETAFIX, WHY DON'T WE ADD A FEW NICE ROAST BOARS?

?!? WHY NOT GO AND CHOP UP SOME KINDLING FOR THE FIRE, OBELIX?

WELL, I ONLY THOUGHT HE'D GONE AND FORGOTTEN THE BOARS...

!

CHOP, CHOP, CHOP, CHOP!

AMAZING! I'VE NEVER SEEN ANYONE CHOP WOOD LIKE THAT BEFORE!

OH, THAT'S NOTHING! I COULD CUT A WHOLE TREE DOWN THAT WAY, ONLY DOGMATIX WOULDN'T LIKE IT!

SOON AFTERWARDS..

READY IN A MOMENT!

I'M A BIT WORRIED, CENTURION! A COUSIN OF MINE STATIONED IN ARMORICA TOLD ME ABOUT A DRUID THERE WHO HAS STRANGE POWERS, AND I'M JUST WONDERING WHETHER...

YOU'VE GOT A POINT, INFECTIUS VIRUS. WE MUST BE CAREFUL!

WOULD YOU LIKE TO TASTE THE SOUP FOR SEASONING, CENTURION?

JUST A MOMENT, GAUL! HOW DO I KNOW YOU'RE NOT TRYING TO POISON THE GARRISON, SO AS TO SET THE PRISONERS FREE?

I QUITE UNDERSTAND YOUR FEELINGS. YOU DON'T WANT TO FIND YOURSELF IN THE SOUP! SO WE'LL DRINK SOME OURSELVES TO SHOW IT'S ALL RIGHT!

AND TO PROVE IT EVEN MORE CONCLUSIVELY, WE'LL GIVE SOME TO THE PRISONERS TOO!

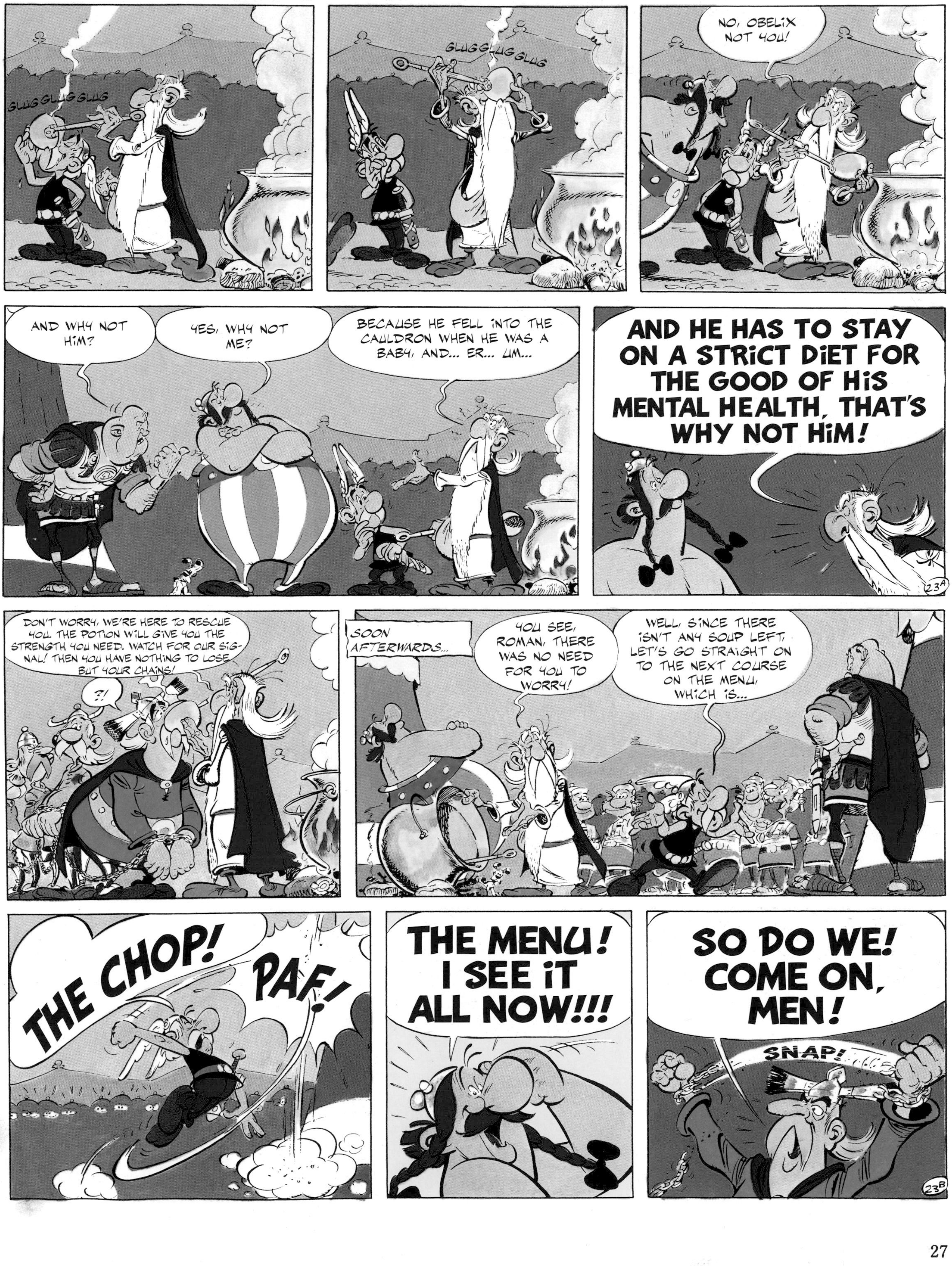
GLUG GLUG GLUG
GLUG GLUG GLUG
NO, OBELIX NOT YOU!
AND WHY NOT HIM?
YES, WHY NOT ME?
BECAUSE HE FELL INTO THE CAULDRON WHEN HE WAS A BABY, AND... ER... UM...
AND HE HAS TO STAY ON A STRICT DIET FOR THE GOOD OF HIS MENTAL HEALTH, THAT'S WHY NOT HIM!
DON'T WORRY, WE'RE HERE TO RESCUE YOU. THE POTION WILL GIVE YOU THE STRENGTH YOU NEED. WATCH FOR OUR SIGNAL! THEN YOU HAVE NOTHING TO LOSE BUT YOUR CHAINS!
?!
SOON AFTERWARDS...
YOU SEE, ROMAN, THERE WAS NO NEED FOR YOU TO WORRY!
WELL, SINCE THERE ISN'T ANY SOUP LEFT, LET'S GO STRAIGHT ON TO THE NEXT COURSE ON THE MENU, WHICH IS...
THE CHOP!
PAF!
THE MENU! I SEE IT ALL NOW!!!
SO DO WE! COME ON, MEN!
SNAP!

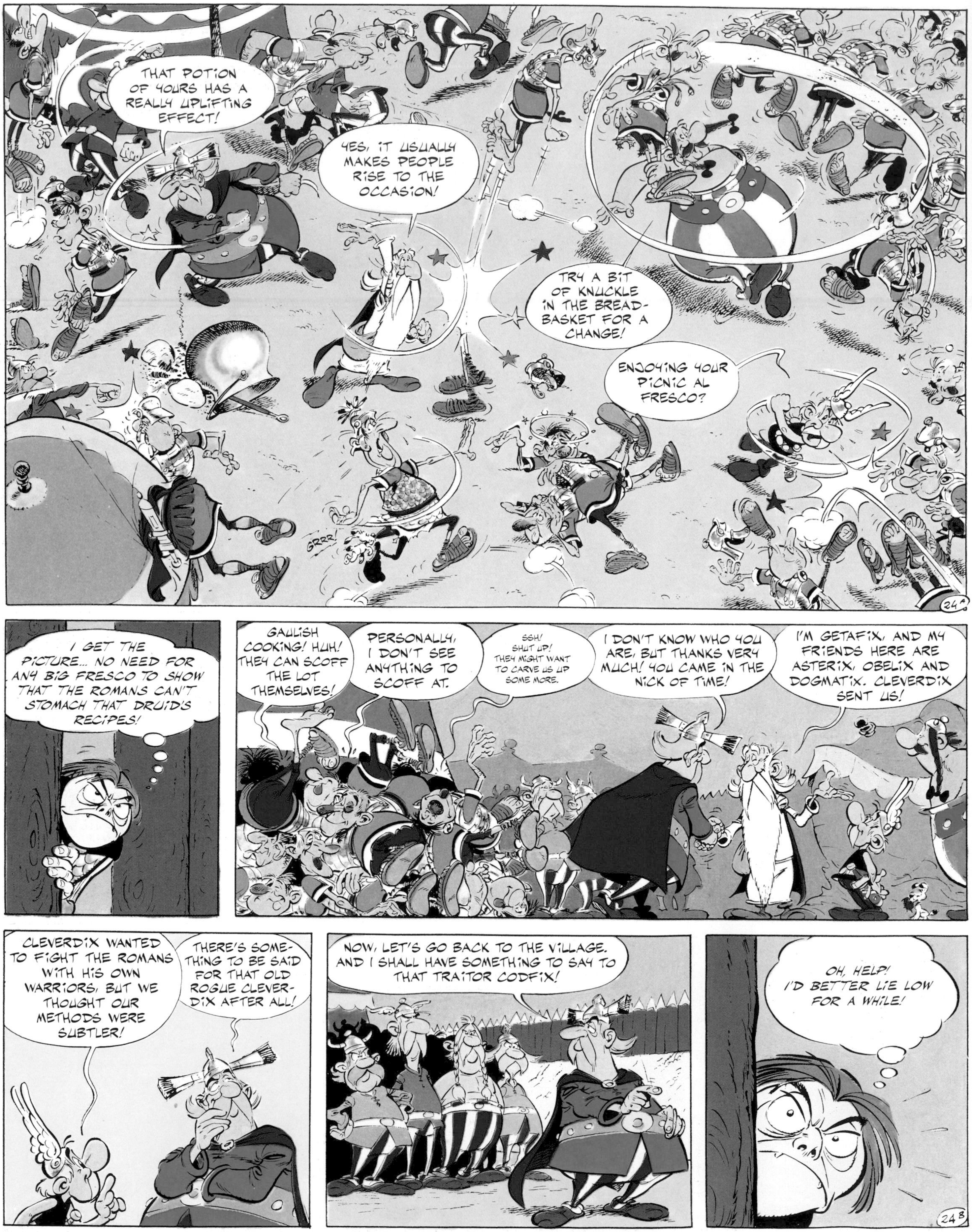

THAT POTION OF YOURS HAS A REALLY UPLIFTING EFFECT!
YES, IT USUALLY MAKES PEOPLE RISE TO THE OCCASION!
TRY A BIT OF KNUCKLE IN THE BREAD-BASKET FOR A CHANGE!
ENJOYING YOUR PICNIC AL FRESCO?
GRRR!
I GET THE PICTURE... NO NEED FOR ANY BIG FRESCO TO SHOW THAT THE ROMANS CAN'T STOMACH THAT DRUID'S RECIPES!
GAULISH COOKING! HUH! THEY CAN SCOFF THE LOT THEMSELVES!
PERSONALLY, I DON'T SEE ANYTHING TO SCOFF AT.
SSH! SHUT UP! THEY MIGHT WANT TO CARVE US UP SOME MORE.
I DON'T KNOW WHO YOU ARE, BUT THANKS VERY MUCH! YOU CAME IN THE NICK OF TIME!
I'M GETAFIX, AND MY FRIENDS HERE ARE ASTERIX, OBELIX AND DOGMATIX. CLEVERDIX SENT US!
CLEVERDIX WANTED TO FIGHT THE ROMANS WITH HIS OWN WARRIORS, BUT WE THOUGHT OUR METHODS WERE SUBTLER!
THERE'S SOMETHING TO BE SAID FOR THAT OLD ROGUE CLEVERDIX AFTER ALL!
NOW, LET'S GO BACK TO THE VILLAGE. AND I SHALL HAVE SOMETHING TO SAY TO THAT TRAITOR CODFIX!
OH, HELP! I'D BETTER LIE LOW FOR A WHILE!

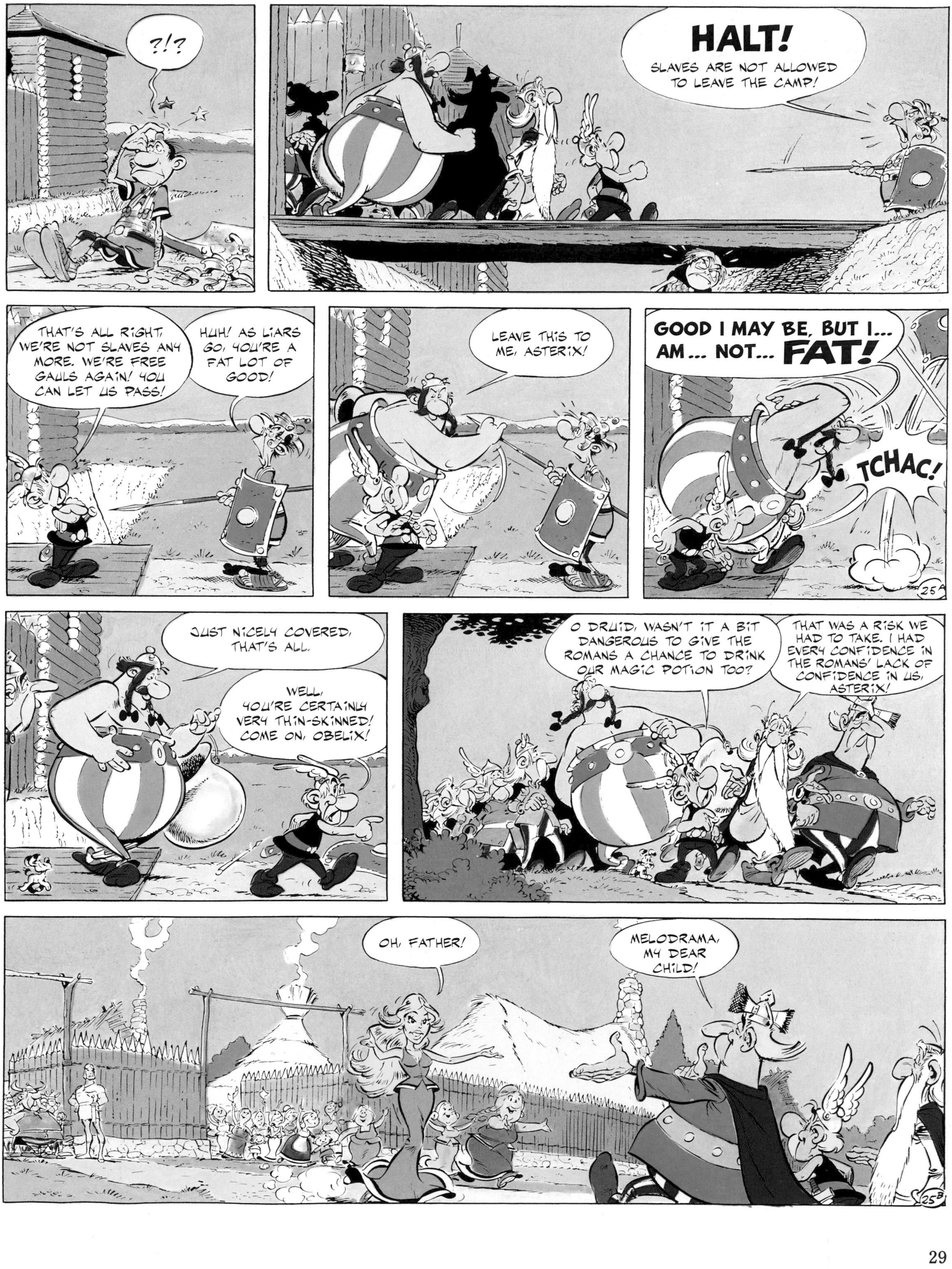
?!?
HALT!
SLAVES ARE NOT ALLOWED TO LEAVE THE CAMP!
THAT'S ALL RIGHT, WE'RE NOT SLAVES ANY MORE. WE'RE FREE GAULS AGAIN! YOU CAN LET US PASS!
HUH! AS LIARS GO, YOU'RE A FAT LOT OF GOOD!
LEAVE THIS TO ME, ASTERIX!
GOOD I MAY BE, BUT I... AM... NOT... FAT!
TCHAC!
JUST NICELY COVERED, THAT'S ALL.
WELL, YOU'RE CERTAINLY VERY THIN-SKINNED! COME ON, OBELIX!
O DRUID, WASN'T IT A BIT DANGEROUS TO GIVE THE ROMANS A CHANCE TO DRINK OUR MAGIC POTION TOO?
THAT WAS A RISK WE HAD TO TAKE. I HAD EVERY CONFIDENCE IN THE ROMANS' LACK OF CONFIDENCE IN US, ASTERIX!
OH, FATHER!
MELODRAMA, MY DEAR CHILD!

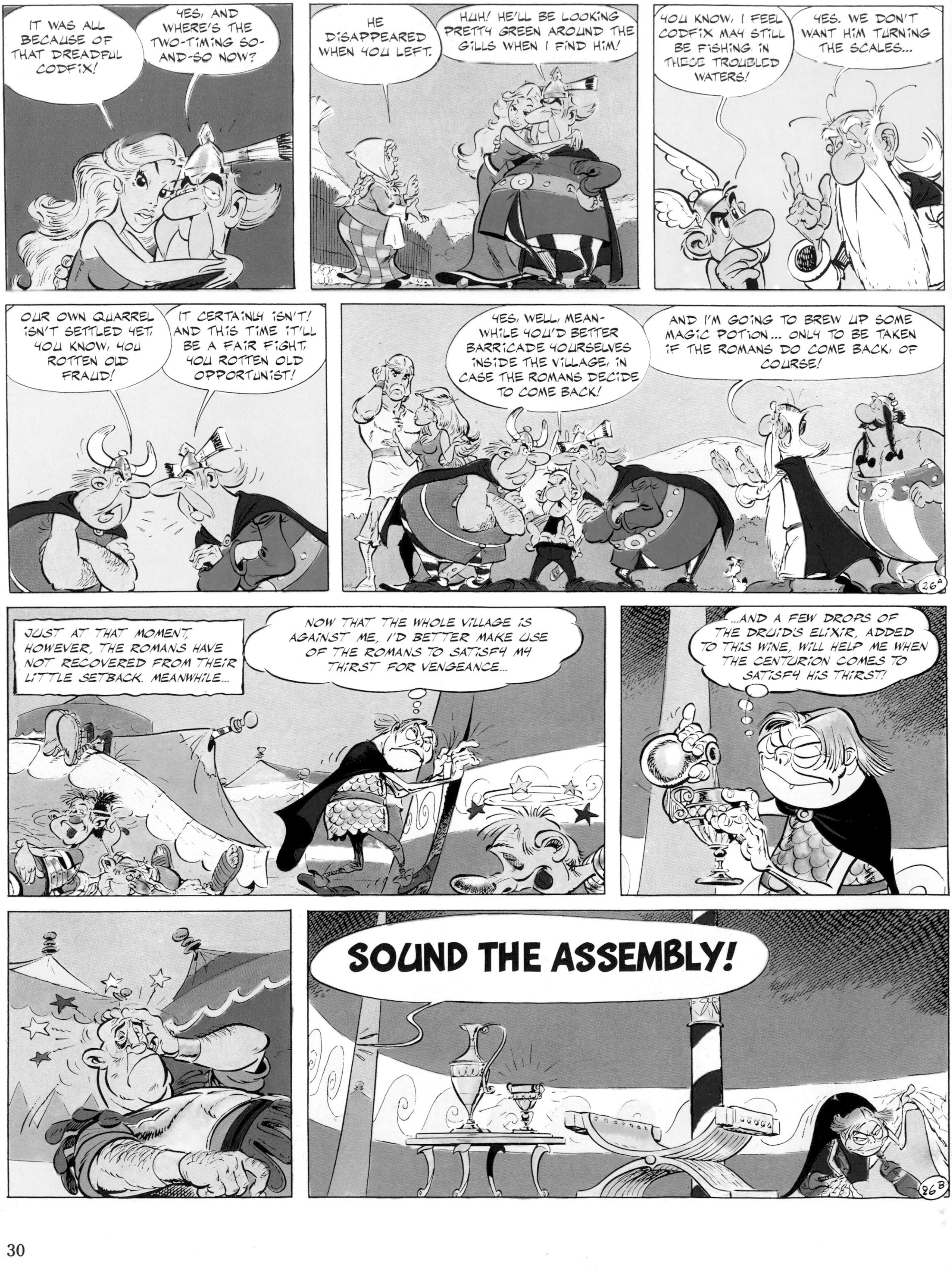
IT WAS ALL BECAUSE OF THAT DREADFUL CODFIX!
YES, AND WHERE'S THE TWO-TIMING SO-AND-SO NOW?
HE DISAPPEARED WHEN YOU LEFT.
HUH! HE'LL BE LOOKING PRETTY GREEN AROUND THE GILLS WHEN I FIND HIM!
YOU KNOW, I FEEL CODFIX MAY STILL BE FISHING IN THESE TROUBLED WATERS!
YES. WE DON'T WANT HIM TURNING THE SCALES...
OUR OWN QUARREL ISN'T SETTLED YET, YOU KNOW, YOU ROTTEN OLD FRAUD!
IT CERTAINLY ISN'T! AND THIS TIME IT'LL BE A FAIR FIGHT, YOU ROTTEN OLD OPPORTUNIST!
YES, WELL, MEANWHILE YOU'D BETTER BARRICADE YOURSELVES INSIDE THE VILLAGE, IN CASE THE ROMANS DECIDE TO COME BACK!
AND I'M GOING TO BREW UP SOME MAGIC POTION... ONLY TO BE TAKEN IF THE ROMANS DO COME BACK, OF COURSE!
26A
JUST AT THAT MOMENT, HOWEVER, THE ROMANS HAVE NOT RECOVERED FROM THEIR LITTLE SETBACK. MEANWHILE...
NOW THAT THE WHOLE VILLAGE IS AGAINST ME, I'D BETTER MAKE USE OF THE ROMANS TO SATISFY MY THIRST FOR VENGEANCE...
...AND A FEW DROPS OF THE DRUID'S ELIXIR, ADDED TO THIS WINE, WILL HELP ME WHEN THE CENTURION COMES TO SATISFY HIS THIRST!
SOUND THE ASSEMBLY!
26B

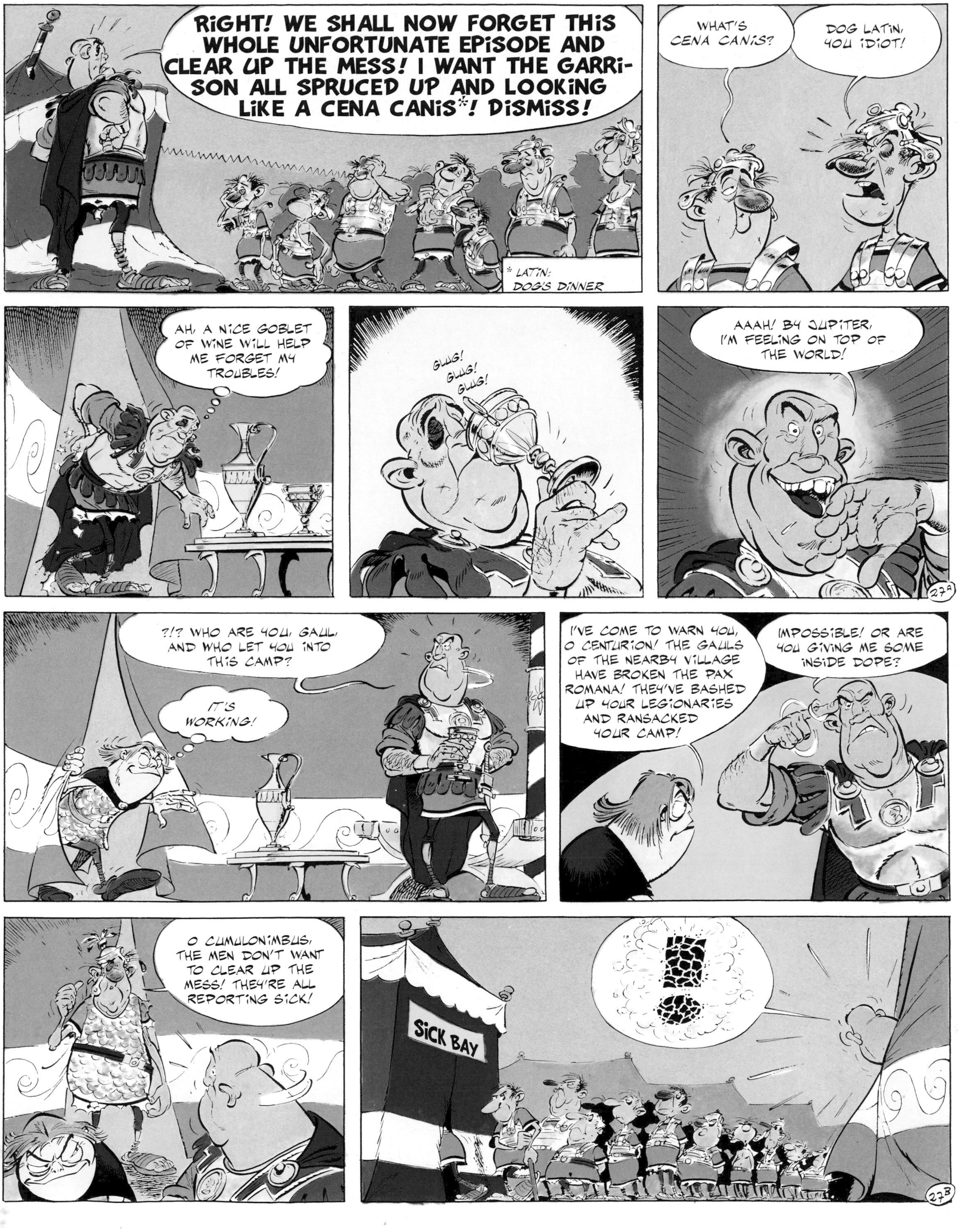
RIGHT! WE SHALL NOW FORGET THIS WHOLE UNFORTUNATE EPISODE AND CLEAR UP THE MESS! I WANT THE GARRISON ALL SPRUCED UP AND LOOKING LIKE A CENA CANIS*! DISMISS!
* LATIN: DOG'S DINNER
WHAT'S CENA CANIS?
DOG LATIN, YOU IDIOT!
AH, A NICE GOBLET OF WINE WILL HELP ME FORGET MY TROUBLES!
GLUG! GLUG! GLUG!
AAAH! BY JUPITER, I'M FEELING ON TOP OF THE WORLD!
27A
?!? WHO ARE YOU, GAUL, AND WHO LET YOU INTO THIS CAMP?
IT'S WORKING!
I'VE COME TO WARN YOU, O CENTURION! THE GAULS OF THE NEARBY VILLAGE HAVE BROKEN THE PAX ROMANA! THEY'VE BASHED UP YOUR LEGIONARIES AND RANSACKED YOUR CAMP!
IMPOSSIBLE! OR ARE YOU GIVING ME SOME INSIDE DOPE?
O CUMULONIMBUS, THE MEN DON'T WANT TO CLEAR UP THE MESS! THEY'RE ALL REPORTING SICK!
SICK BAY
!
27B

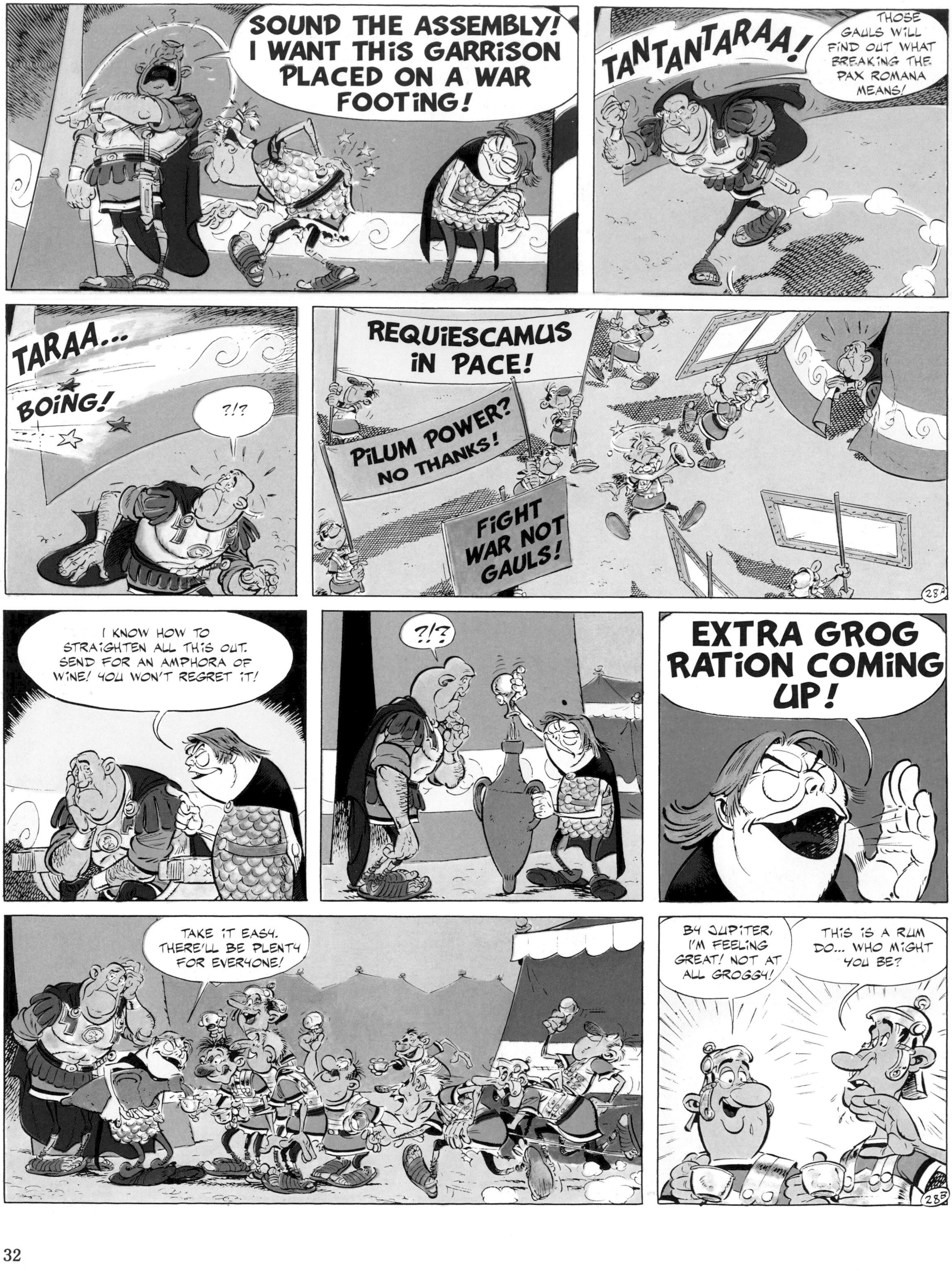
SOUND THE ASSEMBLY! I WANT THIS GARRISON PLACED ON A WAR FOOTING!
TANTANTARAA!
THOSE GAULS WILL FIND OUT WHAT BREAKING THE PAX ROMANA MEANS!
TARAA...
BOING!
?!?
REQUIESCAMUS IN PACE!
PILUM POWER? NO THANKS!
FIGHT WAR NOT GAULS!
28A
I KNOW HOW TO STRAIGHTEN ALL THIS OUT. SEND FOR AN AMPHORA OF WINE! YOU WON'T REGRET IT!
?!?
EXTRA GROG RATION COMING UP!
TAKE IT EASY. THERE'LL BE PLENTY FOR EVERYONE!
BY JUPITER, I'M FEELING GREAT! NOT AT ALL GROGGY!
THIS IS A RUM DO... WHO MIGHT YOU BE?
28B

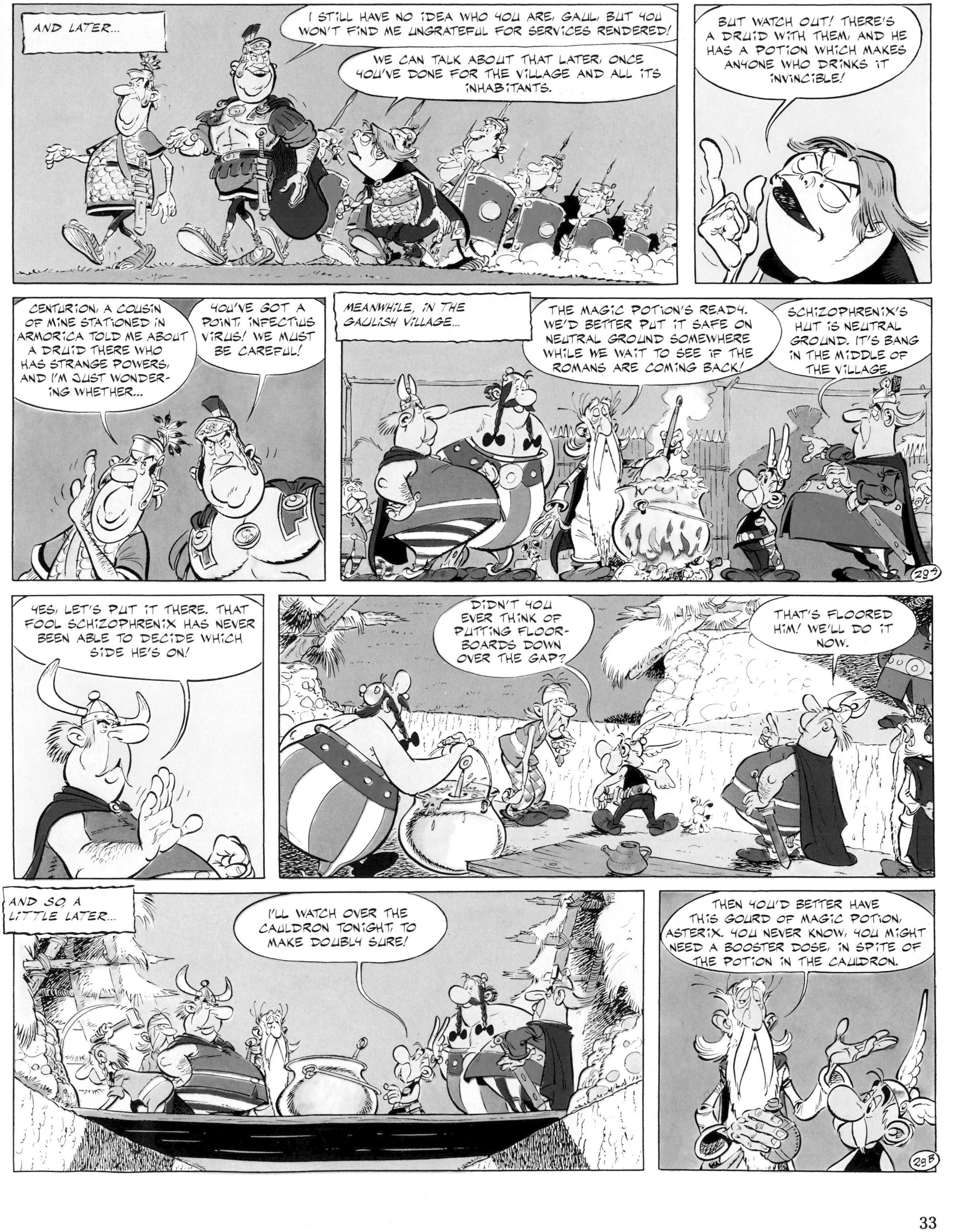

AND LATER...
I STILL HAVE NO IDEA WHO YOU ARE, GAUL, BUT YOU WON'T FIND ME UNGRATEFUL FOR SERVICES RENDERED!
WE CAN TALK ABOUT THAT LATER, ONCE YOU'VE DONE FOR THE VILLAGE AND ALL ITS INHABITANTS.
BUT WATCH OUT! THERE'S A DRUID WITH THEM, AND HE HAS A POTION WHICH MAKES ANYONE WHO DRINKS IT INVINCIBLE!
CENTURION, A COUSIN OF MINE STATIONED IN ARMORICA TOLD ME ABOUT A DRUID THERE WHO HAS STRANGE POWERS, AND I'M JUST WONDERING WHETHER...
YOU'VE GOT A POINT, INFECTIUS VIRUS! WE MUST BE CAREFUL!
MEANWHILE, IN THE GAULISH VILLAGE...
THE MAGIC POTION'S READY. WE'D BETTER PUT IT SAFE ON NEUTRAL GROUND SOMEWHERE WHILE WE WAIT TO SEE IF THE ROMANS ARE COMING BACK!
SCHIZOPHRENIX'S HUT IS NEUTRAL GROUND. IT'S BANG IN THE MIDDLE OF THE VILLAGE.
YES, LET'S PUT IT THERE. THAT FOOL SCHIZOPHRENIX HAS NEVER BEEN ABLE TO DECIDE WHICH SIDE HE'S ON!
DIDN'T YOU EVER THINK OF PUTTING FLOOR-BOARDS DOWN OVER THE GAP?
THAT'S FLOORED HIM! WE'LL DO IT NOW.
AND SO, A LITTLE LATER...
I'LL WATCH OVER THE CAULDRON TONIGHT, TO MAKE DOUBLY SURE!
THEN YOU'D BETTER HAVE THIS GOURD OF MAGIC POTION, ASTERIX. YOU NEVER KNOW, YOU MIGHT NEED A BOOSTER DOSE, IN SPITE OF THE POTION IN THE CAULDRON.

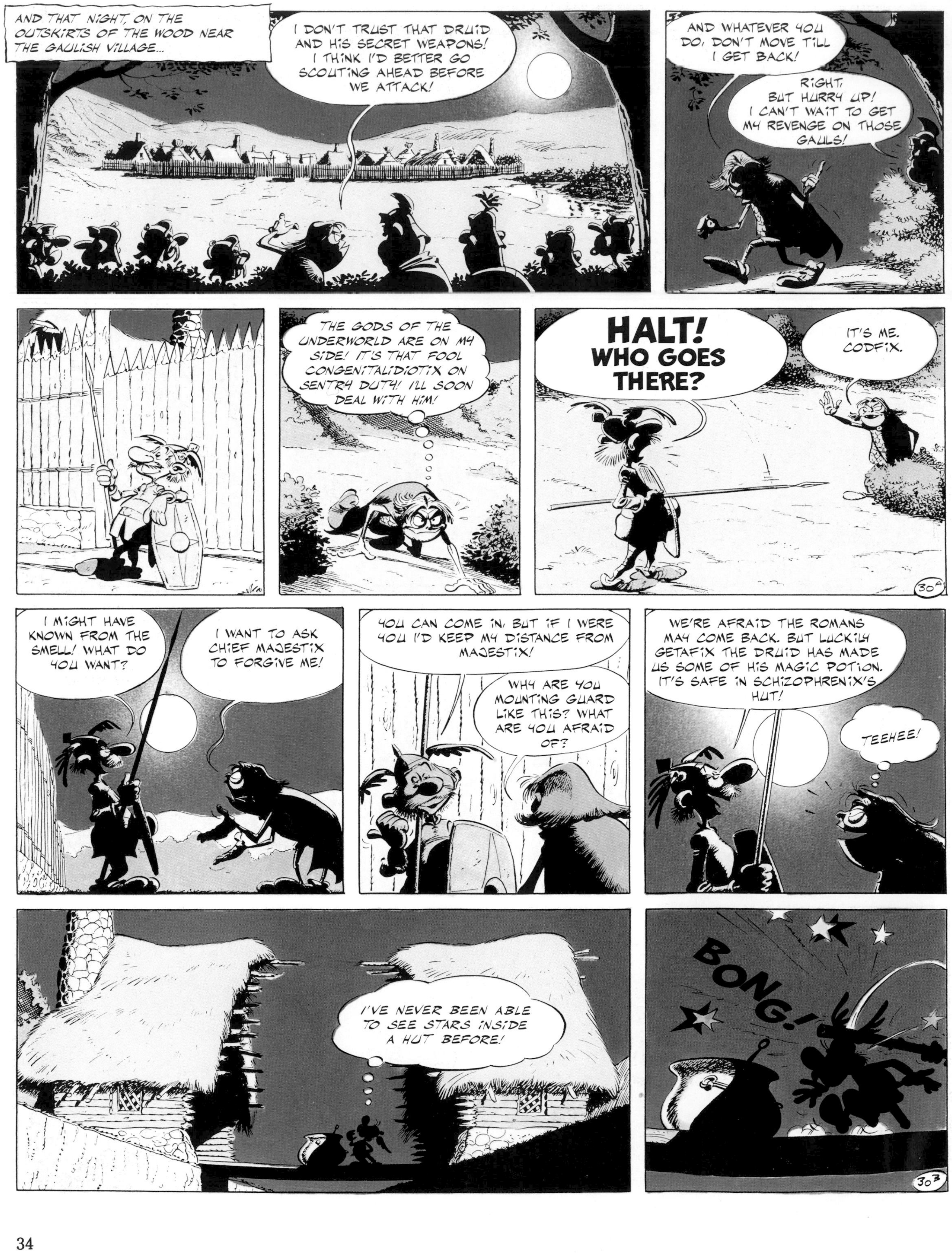
AND THAT NIGHT, ON THE OUTSKIRTS OF THE WOOD NEAR THE GAULISH VILLAGE...
I DON'T TRUST THAT DRUID AND HIS SECRET WEAPONS! I THINK I'D BETTER GO SCOUTING AHEAD BEFORE WE ATTACK!
AND WHATEVER YOU DO, DON'T MOVE TILL I GET BACK!
RIGHT, BUT HURRY UP! I CAN'T WAIT TO GET MY REVENGE ON THOSE GAULS!
THE GODS OF THE UNDERWORLD ARE ON MY SIDE! IT'S THAT FOOL CONGENITALIDIOTIX ON SENTRY DUTY! I'LL SOON DEAL WITH HIM!
HALT! WHO GOES THERE?
IT'S ME. CODFIX.
30A
I MIGHT HAVE KNOWN FROM THE SMELL! WHAT DO YOU WANT?
I WANT TO ASK CHIEF MAJESTIX TO FORGIVE ME!
YOU CAN COME IN, BUT IF I WERE YOU I'D KEEP MY DISTANCE FROM MAJESTIX!
WHY ARE YOU MOUNTING GUARD LIKE THIS? WHAT ARE YOU AFRAID OF?
WE'RE AFRAID THE ROMANS MAY COME BACK. BUT LUCKILY GETAFIX THE DRUID HAS MADE US SOME OF HIS MAGIC POTION. IT'S SAFE IN SCHIZOPHRENIX'S HUT!
TEEHEE!
I'VE NEVER BEEN ABLE TO SEE STARS INSIDE A HUT BEFORE!
BONG!
30B

I'M SURE I SHALL NEED SOME OF THIS!

I FEEL QUITE SORRY FOR CODFIX, APOLOGIZING TO THE CHIEF... HE MUST BE HAVING TO STEEL HIMSELF WONDER IF HE'LL GET AWAY WITH IT?

?!

CRAAASH!

HELP! HELP!

DO SOMETHING, GETAFIX! GIVE HIM SOME OF THE ELIXIR YOU USED ON THE ROMANS!

I'M SORRY, MY DEAR OBELIX, I'M AFRAID I MUST HAVE LEFT IT NEAR THE ROMAN CAMP!

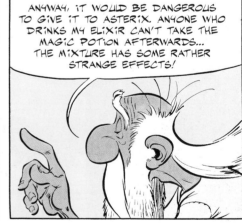

ANYWAY, IT WOULD BE DANGEROUS TO GIVE IT TO ASTERIX. ANYONE WHO DRINKS MY ELIXIR CAN'T TAKE THE MAGIC POTION AFTERWARDS... THE MIXTURE HAS SOME RATHER STRANGE EFFECTS!

BUT LUCKILY ASTERIX IS ALL RIGHT!

THIS TIME I REALLY DO THINK THE SKY HAS FALLEN ON MY HEAD!

THE SKY'S FALLEN ON EVERYONE'S HEAD, ASTERIX! CODFIX HAS STOLEN THE MAGIC POTION, AND HE'S SURE TO DOSE THE ROMANS WITH IT.

HUH! MAGIC POTION OR NO MAGIC POTION, WE CAN DEAL WITH THE ROMANS!

SPOKEN LIKE THE TRUE SON OF A CHIEF!

HMPH!

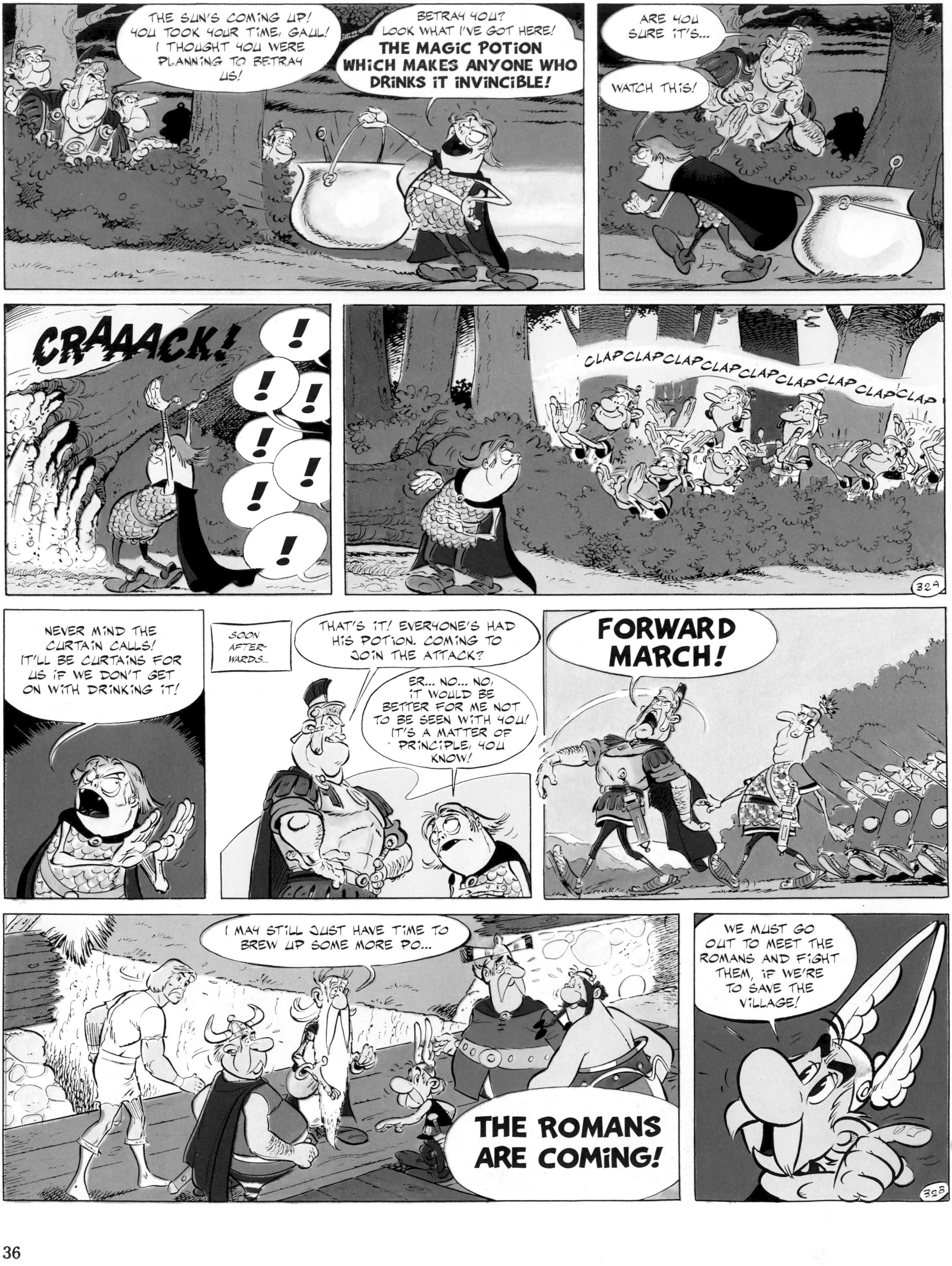

THE SUN'S COMING UP! YOU TOOK YOUR TIME, GAUL! I THOUGHT YOU WERE PLANNING TO BETRAY US!
BETRAY YOU? LOOK WHAT I'VE GOT HERE! THE MAGIC POTION WHICH MAKES ANYONE WHO DRINKS IT INVINCIBLE!
ARE YOU SURE IT'S...
WATCH THIS!
CRAAACK!
!
!
!
!
!
!
!
CLAP CLAP CLAP CLAP CLAP CLAP CLAP CLAP CLAP CLAP
32A
NEVER MIND THE CURTAIN CALLS! IT'LL BE CURTAINS FOR US IF WE DON'T GET ON WITH DRINKING IT!
SOON AFTERWARDS...
THAT'S IT! EVERYONE'S HAD HIS POTION. COMING TO JOIN THE ATTACK?
ER... NO... NO, IT WOULD BE BETTER FOR ME NOT TO BE SEEN WITH YOU! IT'S A MATTER OF PRINCIPLE, YOU KNOW!
FORWARD MARCH!
I MAY STILL JUST HAVE TIME TO BREW UP SOME MORE PO...
THE ROMANS ARE COMING!
WE MUST GO OUT TO MEET THE ROMANS AND FIGHT THEM, IF WE'RE TO SAVE THE VILLAGE!
32B

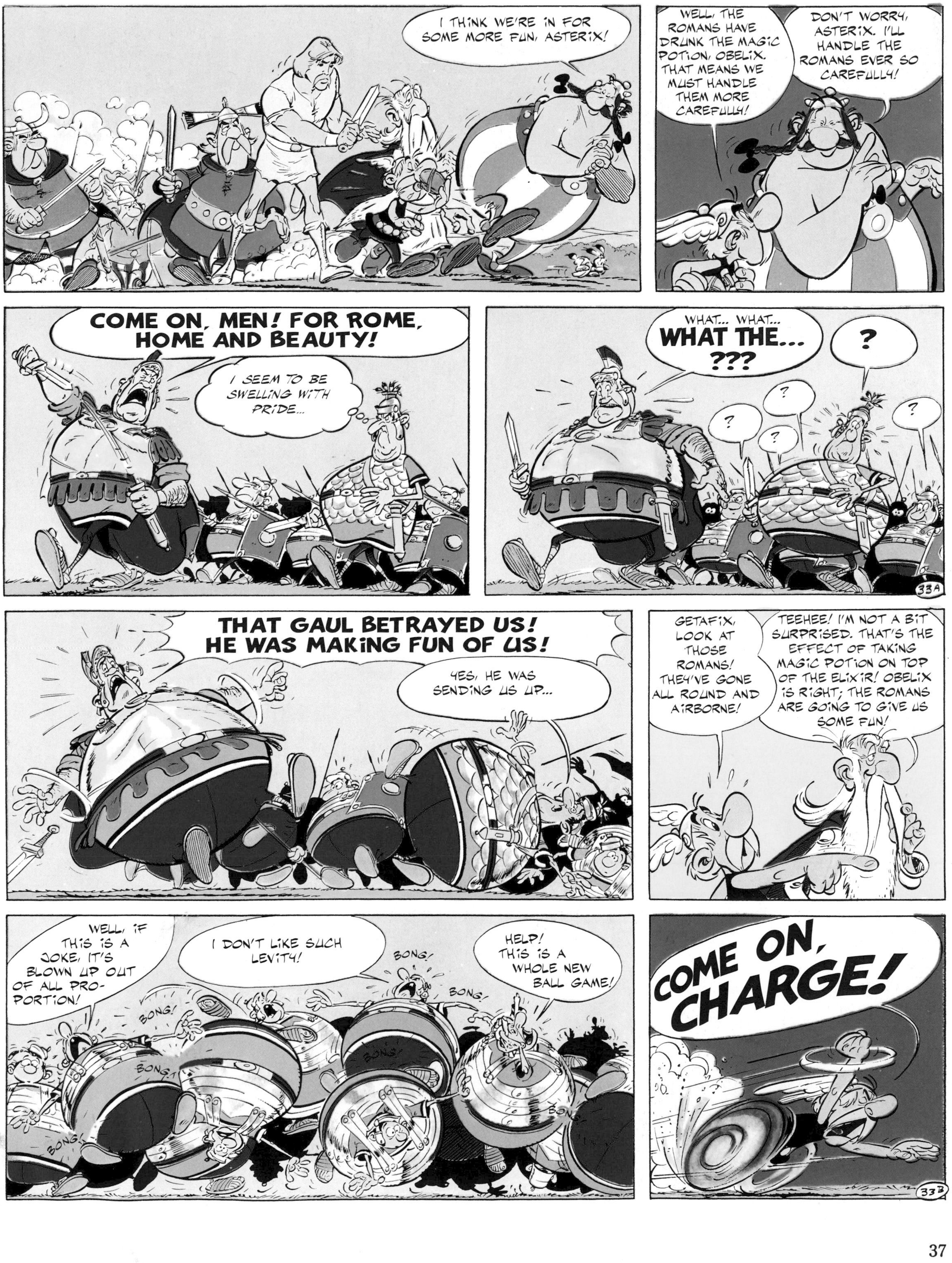
I THINK WE'RE IN FOR SOME MORE FUN, ASTERIX!
WELL, THE ROMANS HAVE DRUNK THE MAGIC POTION, OBELIX. THAT MEANS WE MUST HANDLE THEM MORE CAREFULLY!
DON'T WORRY, ASTERIX. I'LL HANDLE THE ROMANS EVER SO CAREFULLY!
COME ON, MEN! FOR ROME, HOME AND BEAUTY!
I SEEM TO BE SWELLING WITH PRIDE...
WHAT... WHAT... WHAT THE... ???
?
THAT GAUL BETRAYED US! HE WAS MAKING FUN OF US!
YES, HE WAS SENDING US UP...
GETAFIX, LOOK AT THOSE ROMANS! THEY'VE GONE ALL ROUND AND AIRBORNE!
TEEHEE! I'M NOT A BIT SURPRISED. THAT'S THE EFFECT OF TAKING MAGIC POTION ON TOP OF THE ELIXIR! OBELIX IS RIGHT; THE ROMANS ARE GOING TO GIVE US SOME FUN!
WELL, IF THIS IS A JOKE, IT'S BLOWN UP OUT OF ALL PROPORTION!
I DON'T LIKE SUCH LEVITY!
HELP! THIS IS A WHOLE NEW BALL GAME!
BONG!
COME ON, CHARGE!

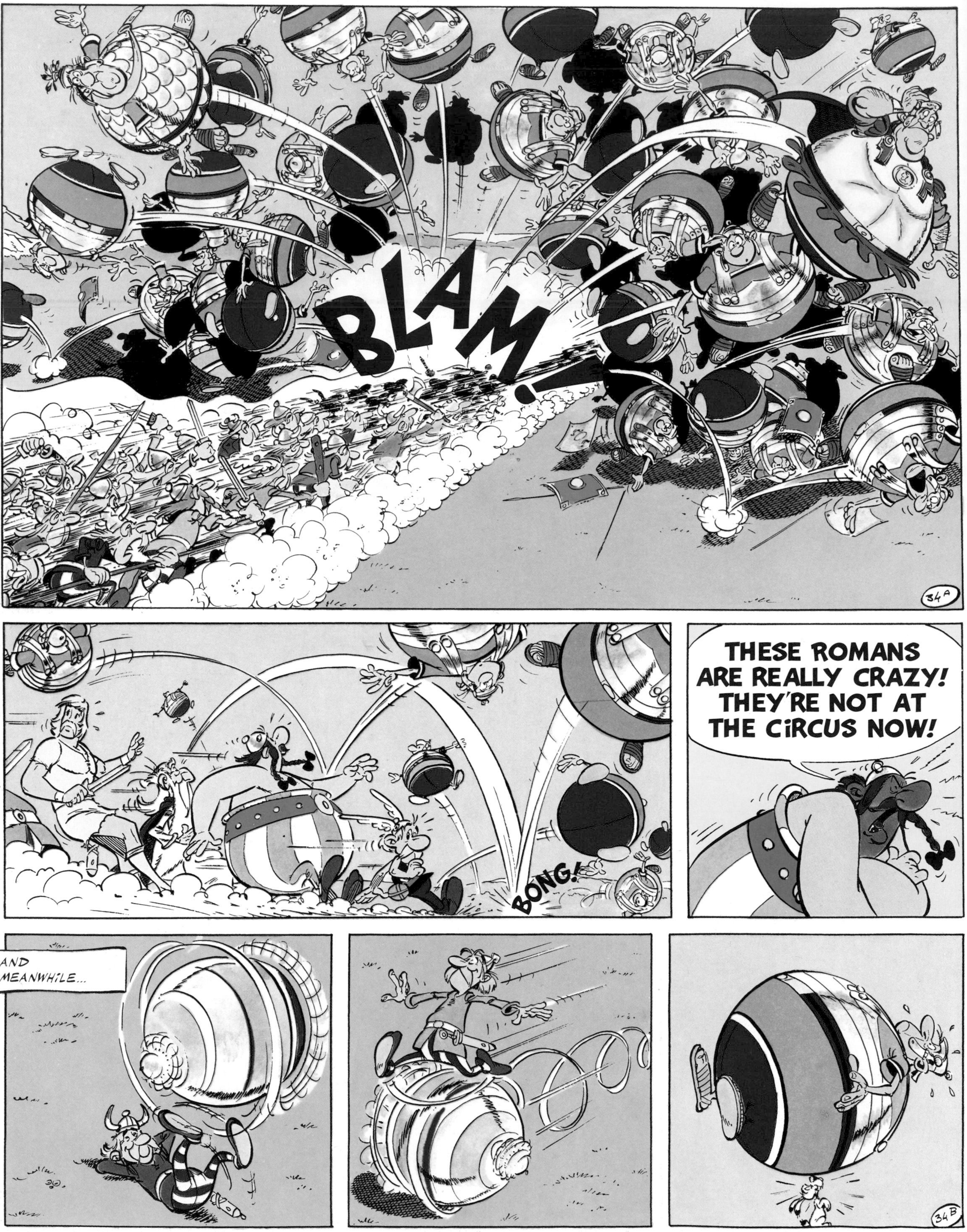
BLAM!
BONG!
THESE ROMANS ARE REALLY CRAZY! THEY'RE NOT AT THE CIRCUS NOW!
AND MEANWHILE...

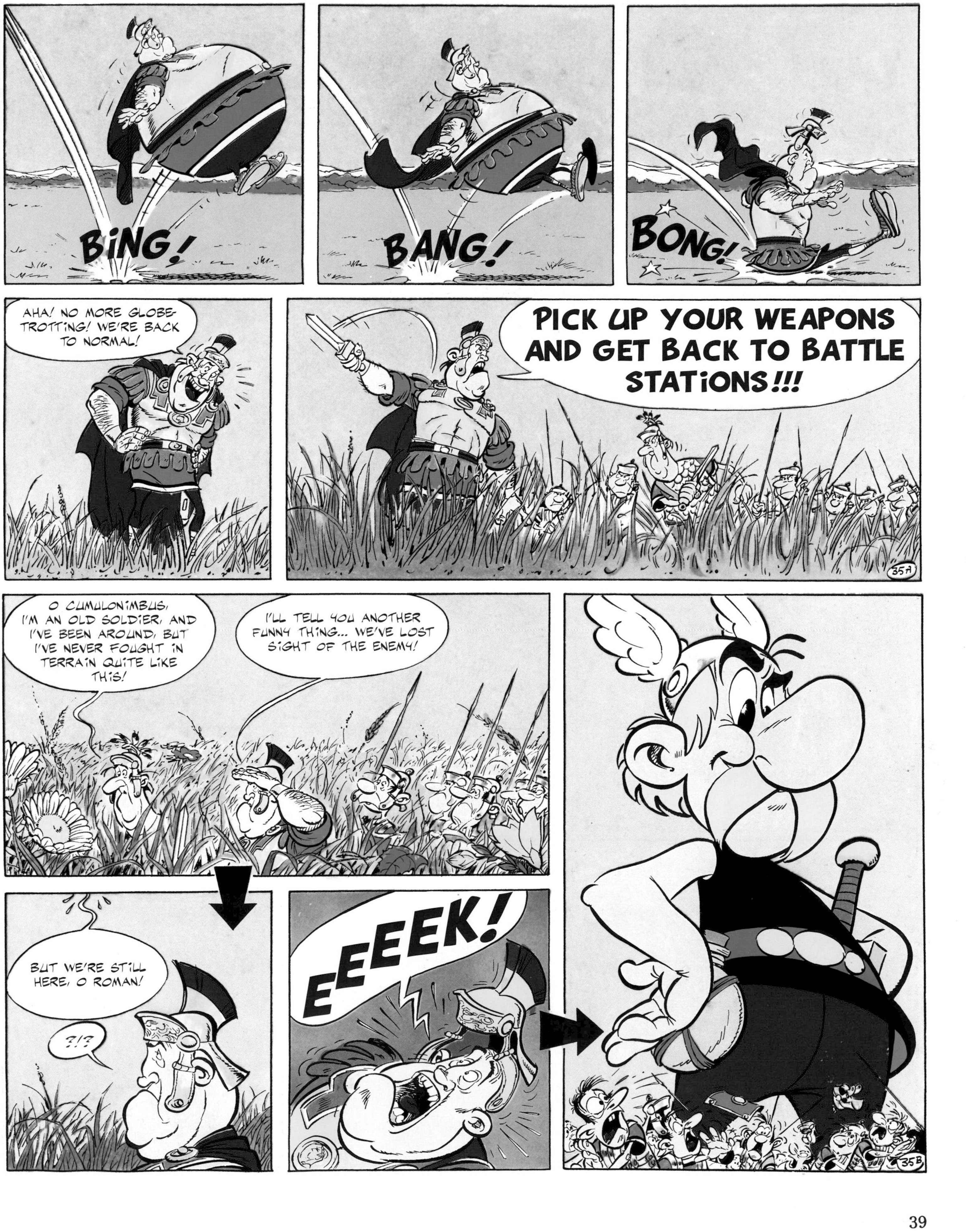
BING!
BANG!
BONG!
AHA! NO MORE GLOBE-TROTTING! WE'RE BACK TO NORMAL!
PICK UP YOUR WEAPONS AND GET BACK TO BATTLE STATIONS!!!
35A
O CUMULONIMBUS, I'M AN OLD SOLDIER, AND I'VE BEEN AROUND, BUT I'VE NEVER FOUGHT IN TERRAIN QUITE LIKE THIS!
I'LL TELL YOU ANOTHER FUNNY THING... WE'VE LOST SIGHT OF THE ENEMY!
BUT WE'RE STILL HERE, O ROMAN!
?!?
EEEEK!
35B

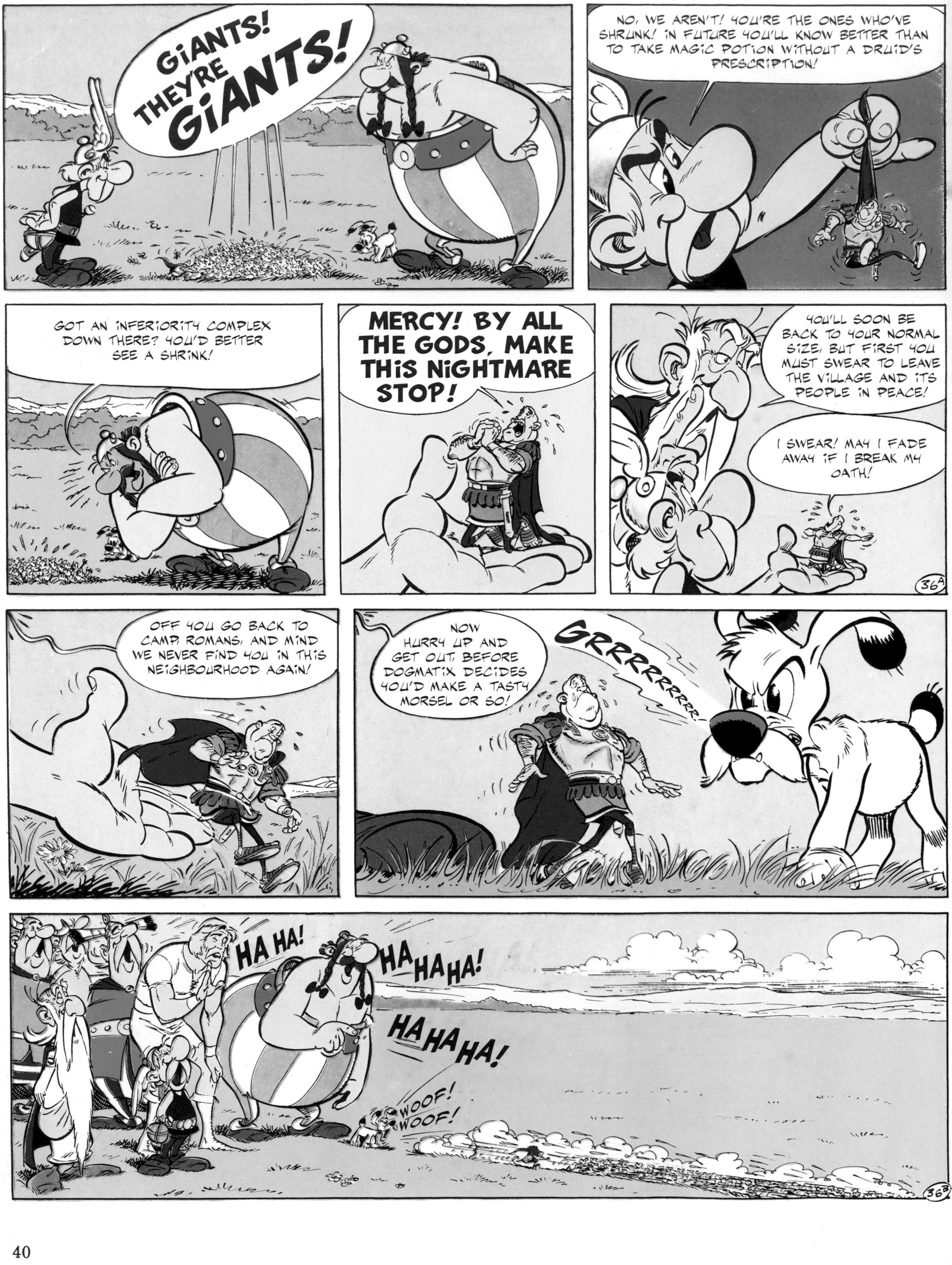
GiANTS! THEY'RE GiANTS!
NO, WE AREN'T! YOU'RE THE ONES WHO'VE SHRUNK! IN FUTURE YOU'LL KNOW BETTER THAN TO TAKE MAGIC POTION WITHOUT A DRUID'S PRESCRIPTION!
GOT AN INFERIORITY COMPLEX DOWN THERE? YOU'D BETTER SEE A SHRINK!
MERCY! BY ALL THE GODS, MAKE THIS NIGHTMARE STOP!
YOU'LL SOON BE BACK TO YOUR NORMAL SIZE, BUT FIRST YOU MUST SWEAR TO LEAVE THE VILLAGE AND ITS PEOPLE IN PEACE!
I SWEAR! MAY I FADE AWAY IF I BREAK MY OATH!
36A
OFF YOU GO BACK TO CAMP, ROMANS, AND MIND WE NEVER FIND YOU IN THIS NEIGHBOURHOOD AGAIN!
NOW HURRY UP AND GET OUT, BEFORE DOGMATIX DECIDES YOU'D MAKE A TASTY MORSEL OR SO!
GRRRRRRRRR!
HA HA!
HA HA HA!
HA HA HA HA!
WOOF! WOOF!
36B

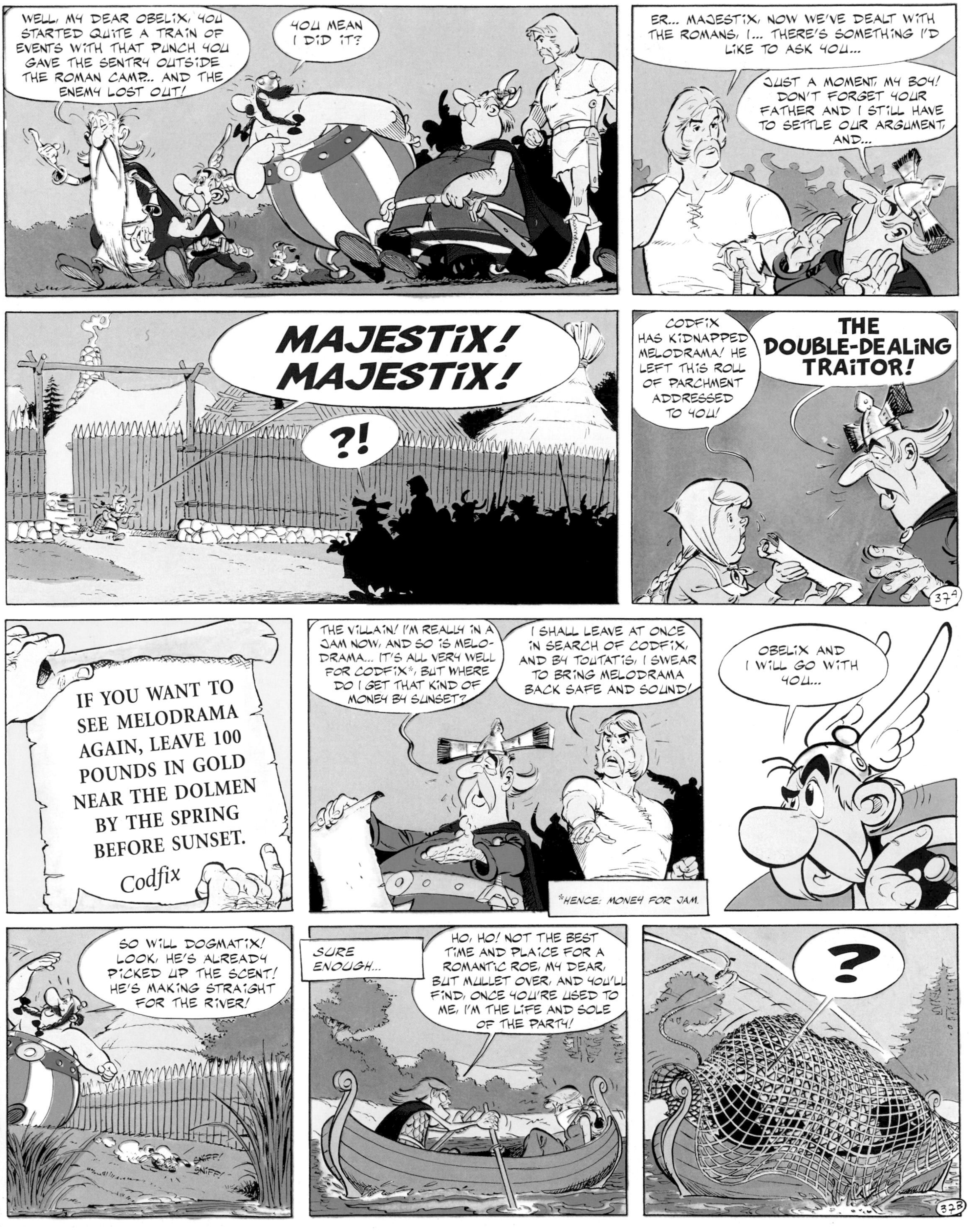
WELL, MY DEAR OBELIX, YOU STARTED QUITE A TRAIN OF EVENTS WITH THAT PUNCH YOU GAVE THE SENTRY OUTSIDE THE ROMAN CAMP.. AND THE ENEMY LOST OUT!
YOU MEAN I DID IT?
ER... MAJESTIX, NOW WE'VE DEALT WITH THE ROMANS, I... THERE'S SOMETHING I'D LIKE TO ASK YOU...
JUST A MOMENT, MY BOY! DON'T FORGET YOUR FATHER AND I STILL HAVE TO SETTLE OUR ARGUMENT, AND...
MAJESTIX! MAJESTIX!
?!
CODFIX HAS KIDNAPPED MELODRAMA! HE LEFT THIS ROLL OF PARCHMENT ADDRESSED TO YOU!
THE DOUBLE-DEALING TRAITOR!
37A
IF YOU WANT TO SEE MELODRAMA AGAIN, LEAVE 100 POUNDS IN GOLD NEAR THE DOLMEN BY THE SPRING BEFORE SUNSET.
Codfix
THE VILLAIN! I'M REALLY IN A JAM NOW, AND SO IS MELODRAMA... IT'S ALL VERY WELL FOR CODFIX*, BUT WHERE DO I GET THAT KIND OF MONEY BY SUNSET?
I SHALL LEAVE AT ONCE IN SEARCH OF CODFIX, AND BY TOUTATIS, I SWEAR TO BRING MELODRAMA BACK SAFE AND SOUND!
*HENCE: MONEY FOR JAM.
OBELIX AND I WILL GO WITH YOU...
SO WILL DOGMATIX! LOOK, HE'S ALREADY PICKED UP THE SCENT! HE'S MAKING STRAIGHT FOR THE RIVER!
SNIFF! SNIFF!
SURE ENOUGH...
HO, HO! NOT THE BEST TIME AND PLAICE FOR A ROMANTIC ROE, MY DEAR, BUT MULLET OVER, AND YOU'LL FIND, ONCE YOU'RE USED TO ME, I'M THE LIFE AND SOLE OF THE PARTY!
?
37B

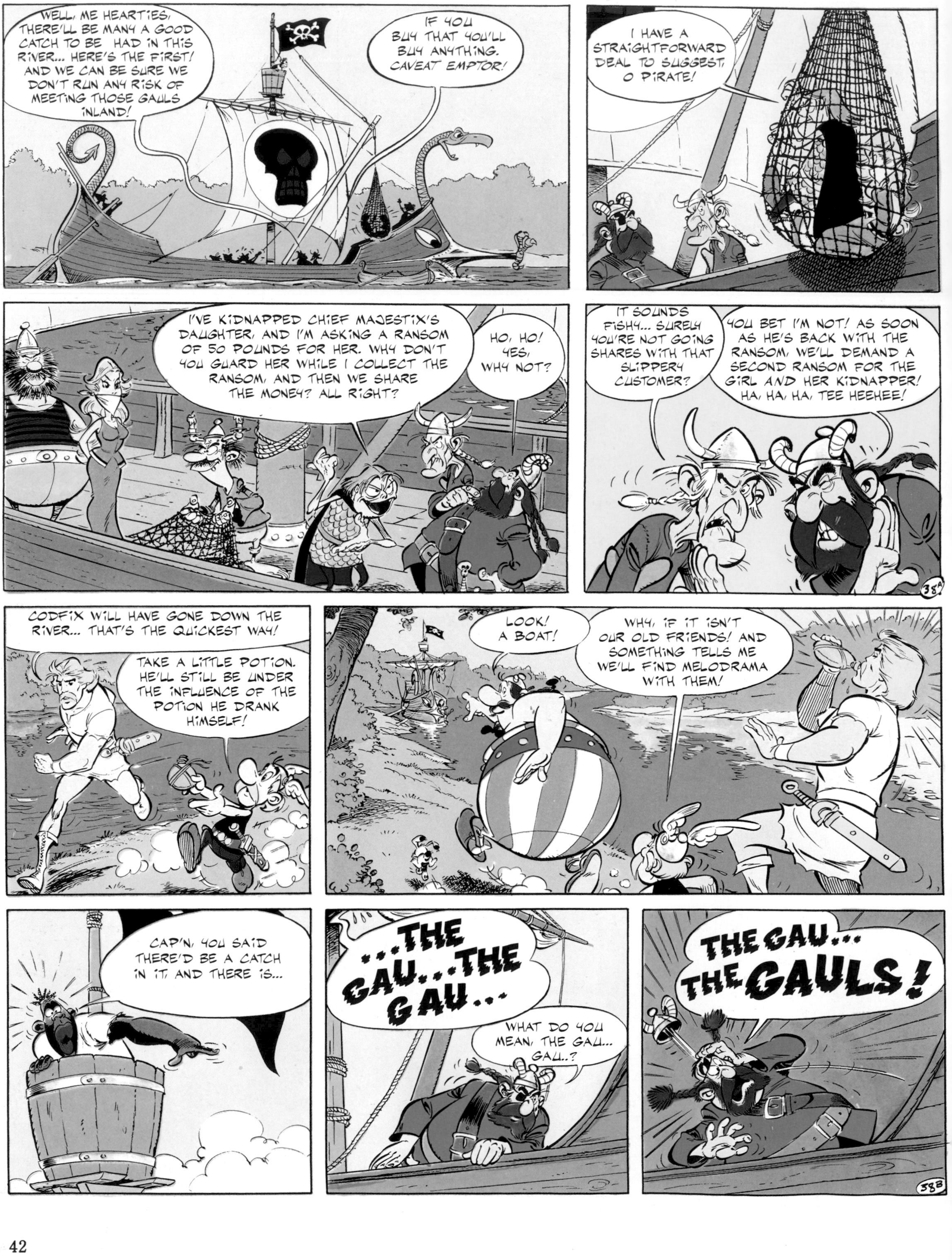
WELL, ME HEARTIES, THERE'LL BE MANY A GOOD CATCH TO BE HAD IN THIS RIVER... HERE'S THE FIRST! AND WE CAN BE SURE WE DON'T RUN ANY RISK OF MEETING THOSE GAULS INLAND!
IF YOU BUY THAT YOU'LL BUY ANYTHING. CAVEAT EMPTOR!
I HAVE A STRAIGHTFORWARD DEAL TO SUGGEST, O PIRATE!
I'VE KIDNAPPED CHIEF MAJESTIX'S DAUGHTER, AND I'M ASKING A RANSOM OF 50 POUNDS FOR HER. WHY DON'T YOU GUARD HER WHILE I COLLECT THE RANSOM, AND THEN WE SHARE THE MONEY? ALL RIGHT?
HO, HO! YES, WHY NOT?
IT SOUNDS FISHY... SURELY YOU'RE NOT GOING SHARES WITH THAT SLIPPERY CUSTOMER?
YOU BET I'M NOT! AS SOON AS HE'S BACK WITH THE RANSOM, WE'LL DEMAND A SECOND RANSOM FOR THE GIRL AND HER KIDNAPPER! HA, HA, HA, TEE HEEHEE!
38A
CODFIX WILL HAVE GONE DOWN THE RIVER... THAT'S THE QUICKEST WAY!
TAKE A LITTLE POTION. HE'LL STILL BE UNDER THE INFLUENCE OF THE POTION HE DRANK HIMSELF!
LOOK! A BOAT!
WHY, IF IT ISN'T OUR OLD FRIENDS! AND SOMETHING TELLS ME WE'LL FIND MELODRAMA WITH THEM!
CAP'N, YOU SAID THERE'D BE A CATCH IN IT, AND THERE IS...
...THE GAU...THE GAU...
WHAT DO YOU MEAN, THE GAU... GAU..?
THE GAU... THE GAULS!
38B

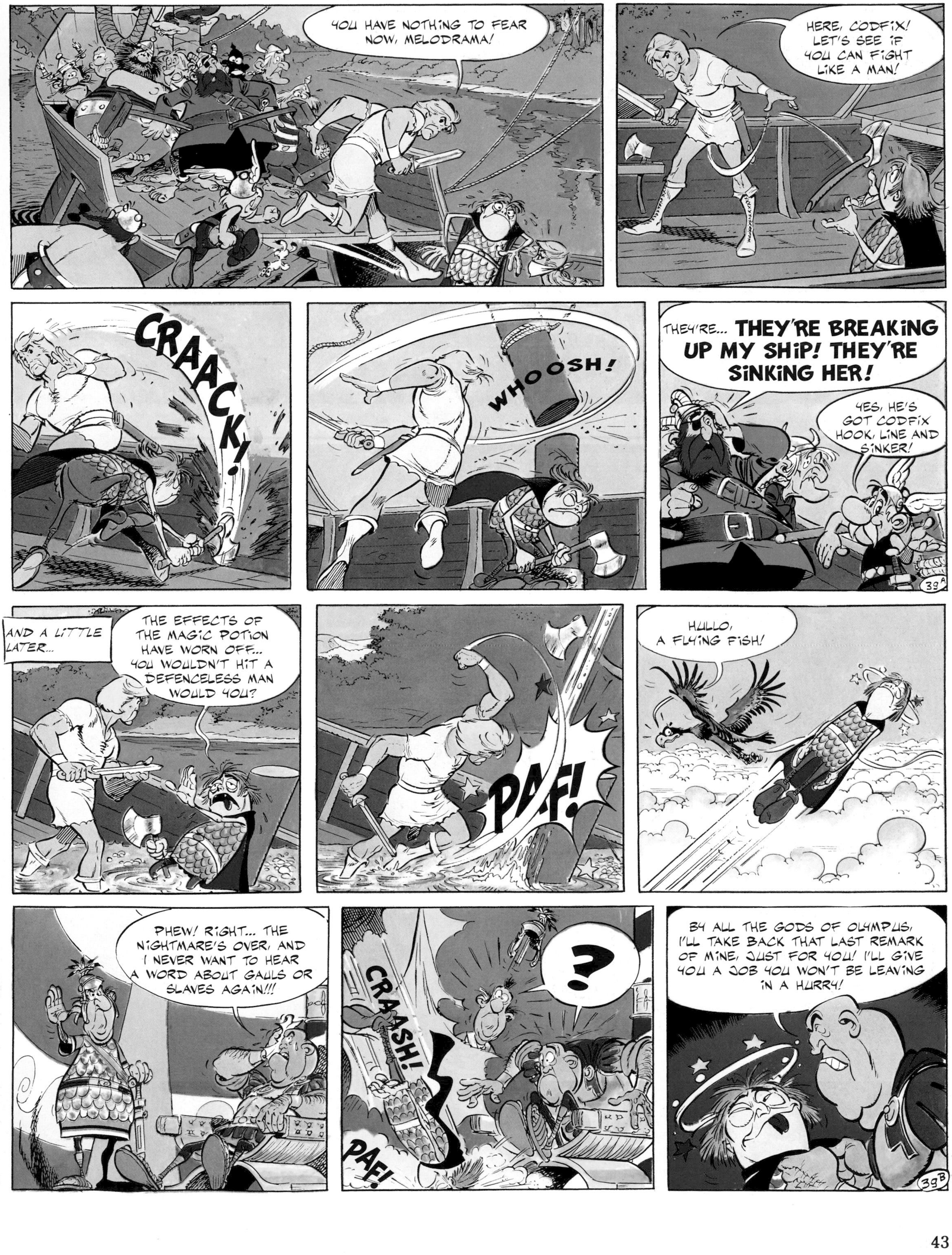
YOU HAVE NOTHING TO FEAR NOW, MELODRAMA!
HERE, CODFIX! LET'S SEE IF YOU CAN FIGHT LIKE A MAN!
CRAACK!
WHOOSH!
THEY'RE... THEY'RE BREAKING UP MY SHIP! THEY'RE SINKING HER!
YES, HE'S GOT CODFIX HOOK, LINE AND SINKER!
39A
AND A LITTLE LATER...
THE EFFECTS OF THE MAGIC POTION HAVE WORN OFF... YOU WOULDN'T HIT A DEFENCELESS MAN WOULD YOU?
PAF!
HULLO, A FLYING FISH!
PHEW! RIGHT... THE NIGHTMARE'S OVER, AND I NEVER WANT TO HEAR A WORD ABOUT GAULS OR SLAVES AGAIN!!!
CRAASH!
PAF!
?
BY ALL THE GODS OF OLYMPUS, I'LL TAKE BACK THAT LAST REMARK OF MINE, JUST FOR YOU! I'LL GIVE YOU A JOB YOU WON'T BE LEAVING IN A HURRY!
39B

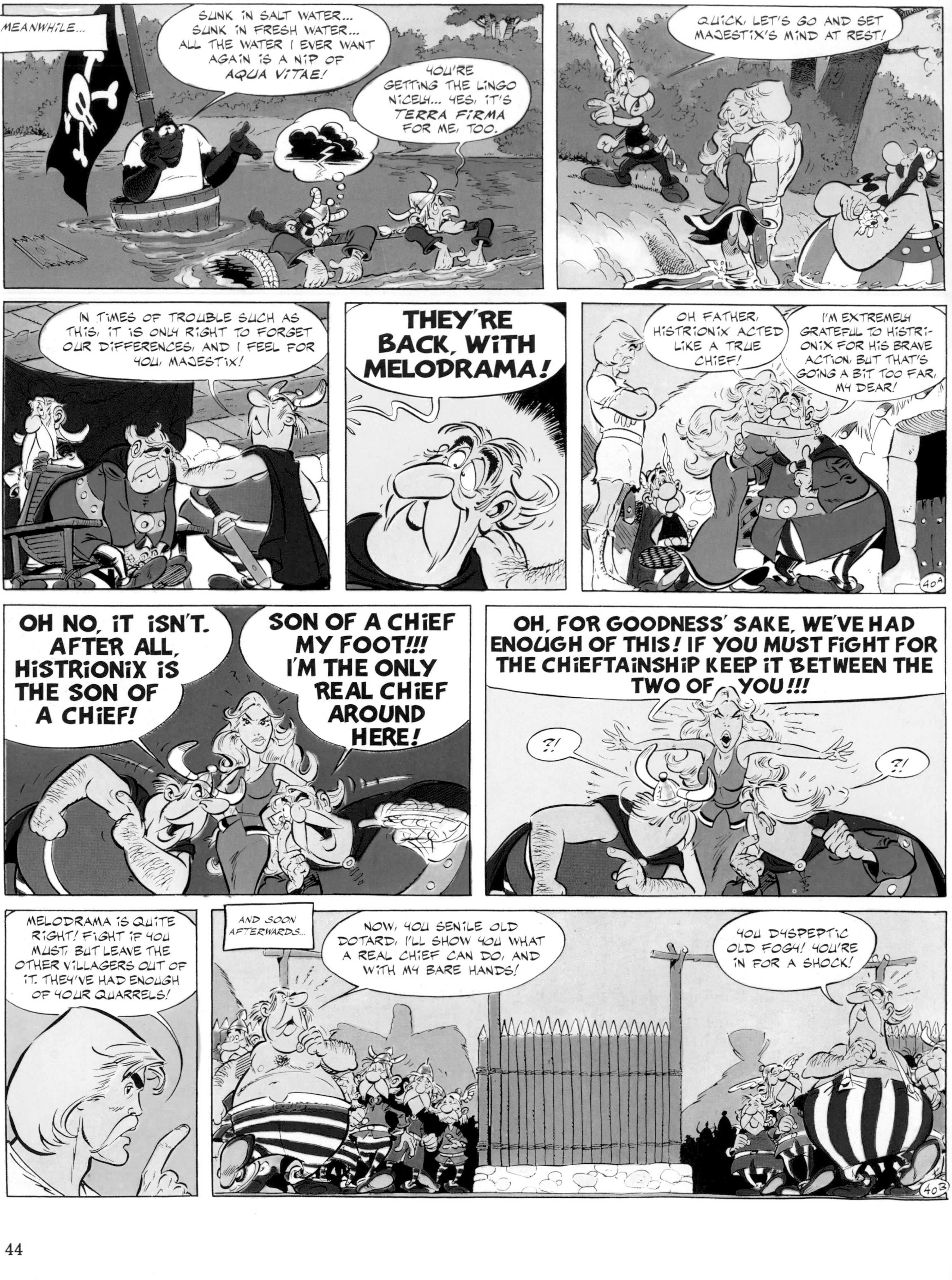
MEANWHILE...
SUNK IN SALT WATER... SUNK IN FRESH WATER... ALL THE WATER I EVER WANT AGAIN IS A NIP OF AQUA VITAE!
YOU'RE GETTING THE LINGO NICELY... YES, IT'S TERRA FIRMA FOR ME, TOO.
QUICK, LET'S GO AND SET MAJESTIX'S MIND AT REST!
IN TIMES OF TROUBLE SUCH AS THIS, IT IS ONLY RIGHT TO FORGET OUR DIFFERENCES, AND I FEEL FOR YOU, MAJESTIX!
THEY'RE BACK, WITH MELODRAMA!
OH FATHER, HISTRIONIX ACTED LIKE A TRUE CHIEF!
I'M EXTREMELY GRATEFUL TO HISTRIONIX FOR HIS BRAVE ACTION, BUT THAT'S GOING A BIT TOO FAR, MY DEAR!
40A
OH NO, IT ISN'T. AFTER ALL, HISTRIONIX IS THE SON OF A CHIEF!
SON OF A CHIEF MY FOOT!!! I'M THE ONLY REAL CHIEF AROUND HERE!
OH, FOR GOODNESS' SAKE, WE'VE HAD ENOUGH OF THIS! IF YOU MUST FIGHT FOR THE CHIEFTAINSHIP KEEP IT BETWEEN THE TWO OF YOU!!!
?!
?!
MELODRAMA IS QUITE RIGHT! FIGHT IF YOU MUST, BUT LEAVE THE OTHER VILLAGERS OUT OF IT. THEY'VE HAD ENOUGH OF YOUR QUARRELS!
AND SOON AFTERWARDS...
NOW, YOU SENILE OLD DOTARD, I'LL SHOW YOU WHAT A REAL CHIEF CAN DO, AND WITH MY BARE HANDS!
YOU DYSPEPTIC OLD FOGY! YOU'RE IN FOR A SHOCK!
40B

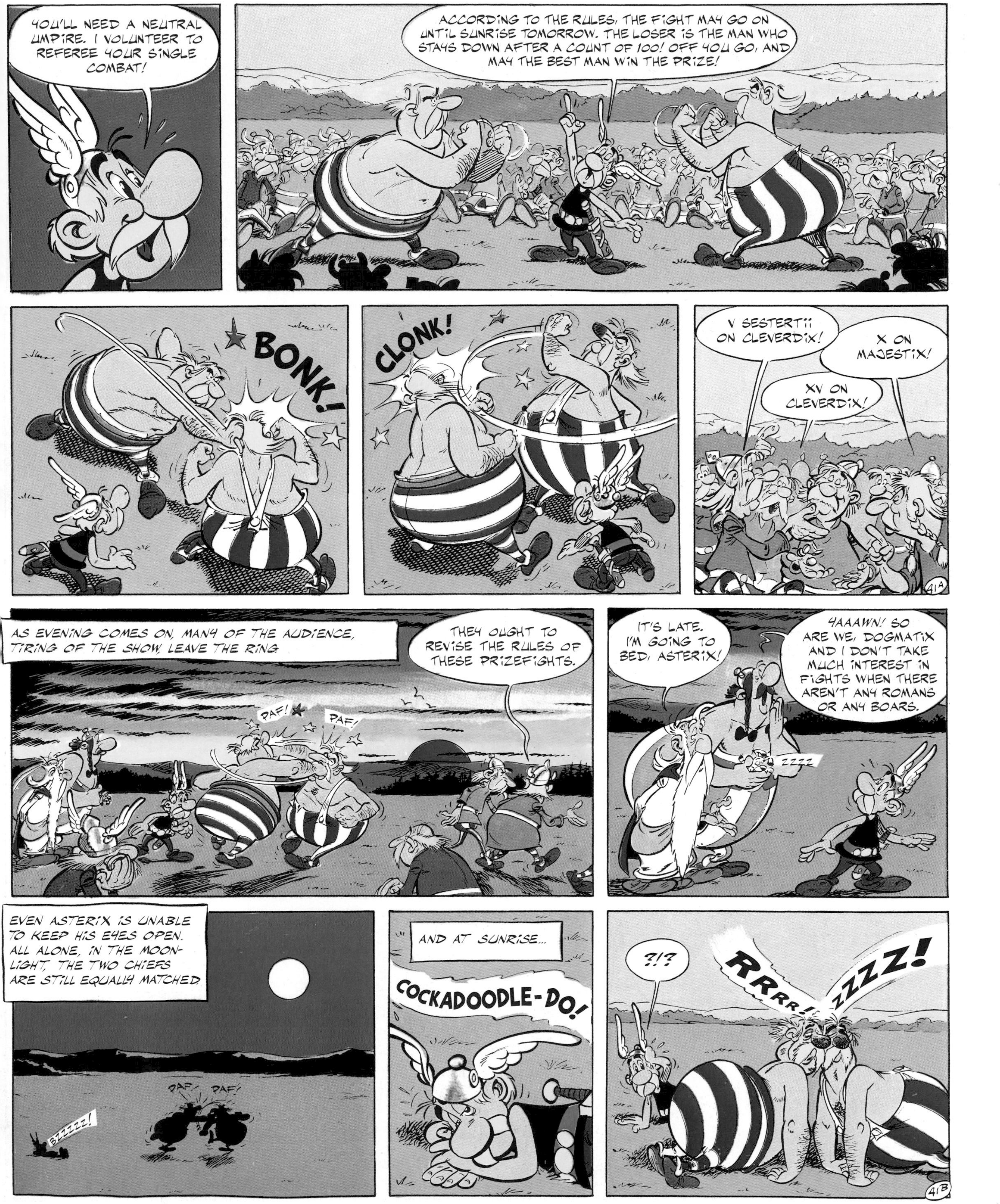

YOU'LL NEED A NEUTRAL UMPIRE. I VOLUNTEER TO REFEREE YOUR SINGLE COMBAT!
ACCORDING TO THE RULES, THE FIGHT MAY GO ON UNTIL SUNRISE TOMORROW. THE LOSER IS THE MAN WHO STAYS DOWN AFTER A COUNT OF 100! OFF YOU GO, AND MAY THE BEST MAN WIN THE PRIZE!
BONK!
CLONK!
V SESTERTII ON CLEVERDIX!
X ON MAJESTIX!
XV ON CLEVERDIX!
AS EVENING COMES ON, MANY OF THE AUDIENCE, TIRING OF THE SHOW, LEAVE THE RING.
THEY OUGHT TO REVISE THE RULES OF THESE PRIZEFIGHTS.
PAF!
PAF!
IT'S LATE. I'M GOING TO BED, ASTERIX!
YAAAWN! SO ARE WE, DOGMATIX AND I DON'T TAKE MUCH INTEREST IN FIGHTS WHEN THERE AREN'T ANY ROMANS OR ANY BOARS.
ZZZZ
EVEN ASTERIX IS UNABLE TO KEEP HIS EYES OPEN. ALL ALONE, IN THE MOONLIGHT, THE TWO CHIEFS ARE STILL EQUALLY MATCHED.
PAF! PAF!
BZZZZZ!
AND AT SUNRISE...
COCKADOODLE-DO!
?!?
RRRRR!
ZZZZ!

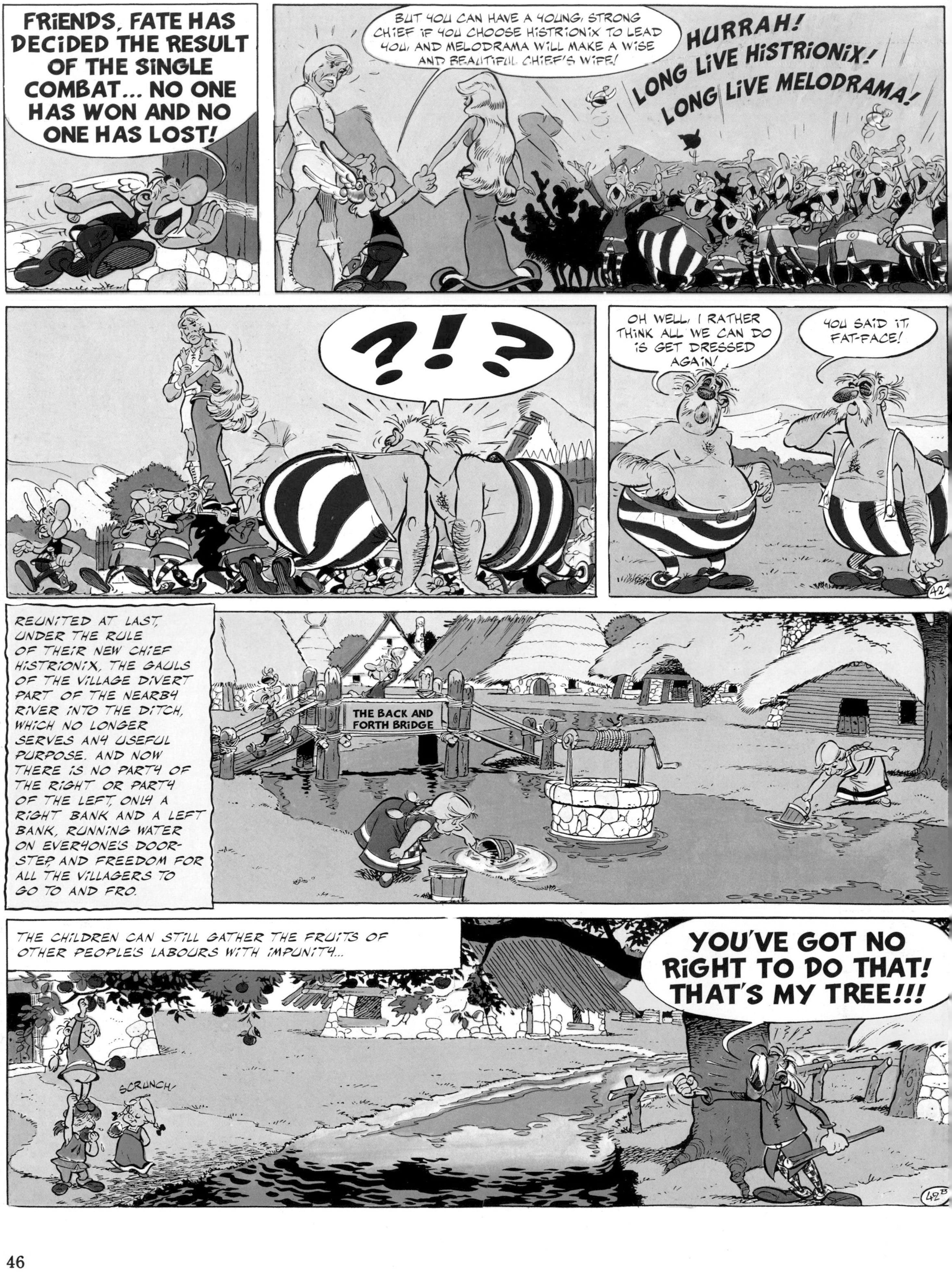
FRIENDS, FATE HAS DECIDED THE RESULT OF THE SINGLE COMBAT... NO ONE HAS WON AND NO ONE HAS LOST!
BUT YOU CAN HAVE A YOUNG, STRONG CHIEF IF YOU CHOOSE HISTRIONIX TO LEAD YOU, AND MELODRAMA WILL MAKE A WISE AND BEAUTIFUL CHIEF'S WIFE!
HURRAH!
LONG LIVE HISTRIONIX!
LONG LIVE MELODRAMA!
?!?
OH WELL, I RATHER THINK ALL WE CAN DO IS GET DRESSED AGAIN!
YOU SAID IT, FAT-FACE!
REUNITED AT LAST, UNDER THE RULE OF THEIR NEW CHIEF HISTRIONIX, THE GAULS OF THE VILLAGE DIVERT PART OF THE NEARBY RIVER INTO THE DITCH, WHICH NO LONGER SERVES ANY USEFUL PURPOSE. AND NOW THERE IS NO PARTY OF THE RIGHT OR PARTY OF THE LEFT, ONLY A RIGHT BANK AND A LEFT BANK, RUNNING WATER ON EVERYONE'S DOORSTEP, AND FREEDOM FOR ALL THE VILLAGERS TO GO TO AND FRO.
THE BACK AND FORTH BRIDGE
THE CHILDREN CAN STILL GATHER THE FRUITS OF OTHER PEOPLE'S LABOURS WITH IMPUNITY...
SCRUNCH!
YOU'VE GOT NO RIGHT TO DO THAT! THAT'S MY TREE!!!

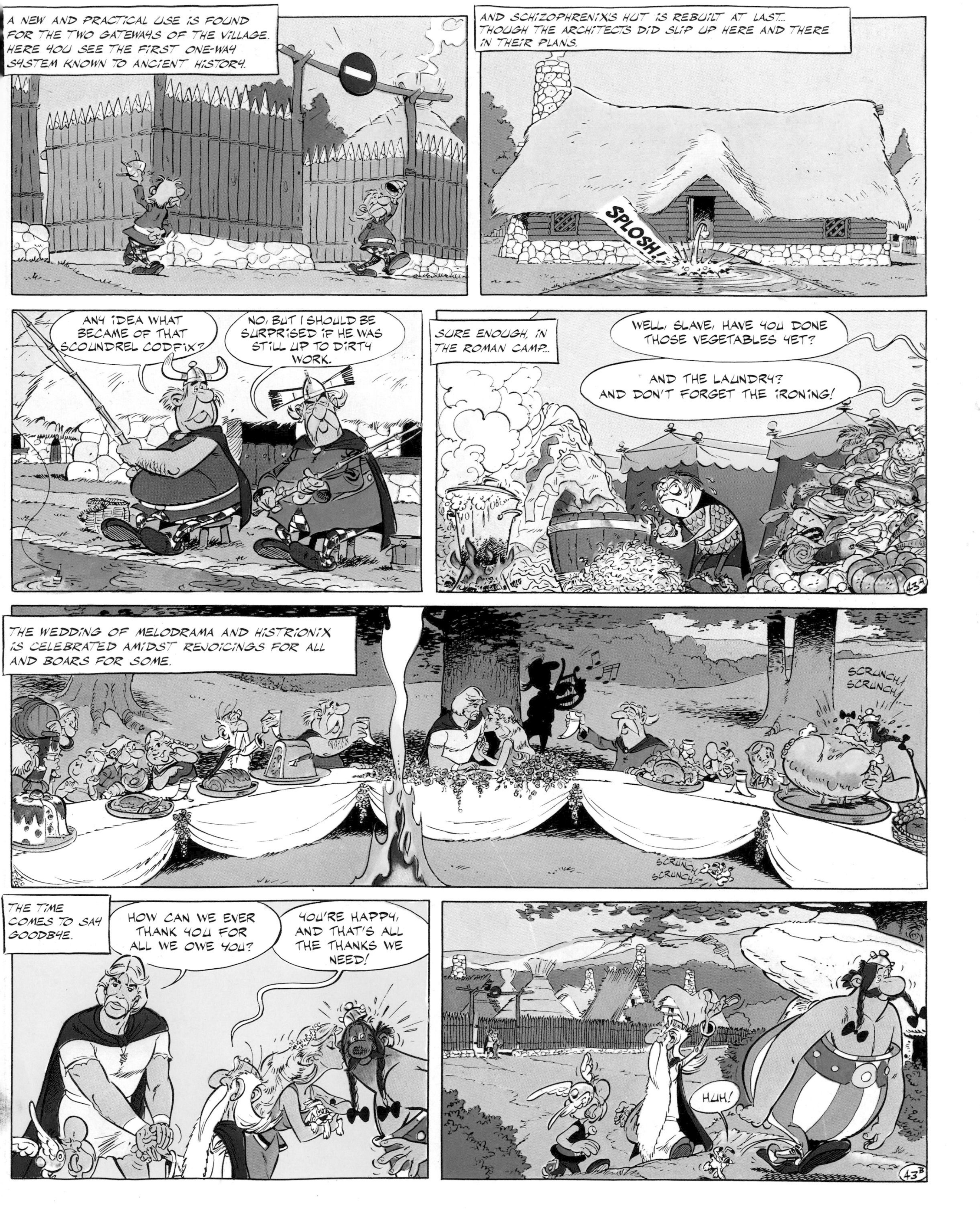

A NEW AND PRACTICAL USE IS FOUND FOR THE TWO GATEWAYS OF THE VILLAGE. HERE YOU SEE THE FIRST ONE-WAY SYSTEM KNOWN TO ANCIENT HISTORY.
AND SCHIZOPHRENIX'S HUT IS REBUILT AT LAST... THOUGH THE ARCHITECTS DID SLIP UP HERE AND THERE IN THEIR PLANS.
SPLOSH!
ANY IDEA WHAT BECAME OF THAT SCOUNDREL CODFIX?
NO, BUT I SHOULD BE SURPRISED IF HE WAS STILL UP TO DIRTY WORK.
SURE ENOUGH, IN THE ROMAN CAMP...
WELL, SLAVE, HAVE YOU DONE THOSE VEGETABLES YET?
AND THE LAUNDRY? AND DON'T FORGET THE IRONING!
THE WEDDING OF MELODRAMA AND HISTRIONIX IS CELEBRATED AMIDST REJOICINGS FOR ALL AND BOARS FOR SOME.
SCRUNCH! SCRUNCH!
SCRUNCH! SCRUNCH!
THE TIME COMES TO SAY GOODBYE.
HOW CAN WE EVER THANK YOU FOR ALL WE OWE YOU?
YOU'RE HAPPY, AND THAT'S ALL THE THANKS WE NEED!
HUH!

LOOK HERE, OBELIX, IT'S THREE DAYS SINCE WE LEFT OUR FRIENDS' VILLAGE, AND YOU HAVEN'T UTTERED A SINGLE WORD! WHAT'S THE MATTER?
BOOHOOHOO! I GET UPSET BY LOVE STORIES WITH HAPPY ENDINGS TOO!
!?!
HUH!
HOWEVER, THE PLEASURES OF HOME-COMING OVERSHADOW ALL OTHER EMOTIONS.
HOW NICE TO BE BACK IN THE CALM AND PEACEFUL ATMOSPHERE OF OUR OWN VILLAGE!
YES, I CAN ALREADY SMELL BOARS ROASTING ON THE SPIT FOR US!
WOOF!
SPLATCH!
44A
AND FOR THE XXVTH TIME, UNDER THE STARRY SKY RULED BY THE GOD TOUTATIS, THE PEOPLE OF ASTERIX'S VILLAGE HAPPILY CELEBRATE THE RETURN OF THEIR HEROES WITH THE TRADITIONAL AND INDISPENSABLE BANQUET.
ALL THAT ABOUT THE GREAT DIVIDE REALLY DOES SOUND MOST IMPROBABLE!
YES... IT WAS SO RIDICULOUS I DARE SAY FUTURE GENERATIONS WILL NEVER BELIEVE A WORD OF IT!
TU-WHOO
SCRUNCH! SCRUNCH!
THE END
UDERZO
44B